THE
SONGS OF
BETTY BAACH

A NOVEL

GLENN TAYLOR

UNIVERSITY OF MASSACHUSETTS PRESS

AMHERST AND BOSTON

ISBN 978-1-62534-730-5 (paper)

Designed by Deste Roosa
Set in Donald and Adobe Caslon Pro

Cover design by adam b. bohannon
Cover art by Glenn Taylor, *Radio Dials,* 2022. Courtesy of the artist.

Library of Congress Cataloging-in-Publication Data
Names: Taylor, M. Glenn, author.
Title: The songs of Betty Baach / Glenn Taylor.
Description: Amherst : University of Massachusetts Press, [2023] | Series:
Juniper prize for fiction
Identifiers: LCCN 2022045172 (print) | LCCN 2022045173 (ebook) | ISBN
9781625347305 (paperback) | ISBN 9781685750220 (ebook) | ISBN
9781685750237 (epub)
Subjects: LCGFT: Novels.
Classification: LCC PS3620.A9593 S66 2023 (print) | LCC PS3620.A9593
(ebook) | DDC 813/.6—dc23/eng/20221017
LC record available at https://lccn.loc.gov/2022045172
LC ebook record available at https://lccn.loc.gov/2022045173

British Library Cataloguing-in-Publication Data
A catalog record for this book is available from the British Library.

Some called Betty Baach* the Everywhen Woman. She claimed she'd lived for more than three hundred years. She wrote these words down and sometimes spoke them aloud, at her home-place on Freon Hill, in 2038. She referred to them as songs. All stories are songs, she'd always say. *Better start dancin.*

*Betty's last name is pronounced *BAYCH.*

Old women in the night can see.
Some nights I cannot sleep at all.
—*Louise McNeill*

what bird remembers
the songs
the miwok sang?
—*Lucille Clifton*

here is a bandolier
a sack of newspapers
three pennies for a nickel

here is a pistol
go stand guard

i am not a cat
i do not smile

in the morning dark
i will dismantle
your carburetor
—*Cheshire Whitt*

CONTENTS

THE SONGS OF BETTY BAACH

SONG OF THE MULEBIRD

Bend me your ear and I'll tell you a story about everything. There are songs you might remember and places you can see, trees and streetcorners and airplanes and old vehicles and creeks and roads with hairpin turns. Remember the dawn chorus through the window? The littlest birds sang loudest, from the deep bosom. The worm-eating warbler trilled like a bug and the song sparrow sang *boy-oh-boy-put-on-the-kettle*.

No one truthfully knows how many birds remain. Estimates on extinction rates vary and I've got no ornithologist to query. But if you step outside and conduct your own study, I bet the hush in the trees will ring your ears. The hills are alive with the sound of truant birds and the field is quiet as a shell. Out in the deep woods, over the course of an hour, you're liable to hear two or three birdsongs, seldom more. They congregate on high and conversate. I've seen them plain as day through Rimmy's binoculars. I saw a woodpecker. Two goldfinches, a titmouse. I've seen more little birds since the Arrow. I'll tell you about the Arrow another time.

There was an old expression, uttered on occasions of escape: the bird has flown. I tell my grandbabies that the birds have flown to the sun, called there by a radial core of love, and when they ask me, "Won't the birds burn alive, BigMom?" I say, "Yes, that's right, children, and only then will the unknown gods convene their barbecue, licking their greasy fingers and picking their teeth with a snapped muskrat dickbone, raising their goblets to toast our true birth, our beginning anew."

One of my most cherished pastimes is saying such things when a child asks about a bird or a muskrat or a plane or a car. I wouldn't speak aloud that grease-licking dickbone part to my grandbabies of course. Or if I did, I'd say *muskrat baculum*.

If a child spots a worm-eating warbler around these parts, that child is said to be lucky. This luck lasts for some undefined short burst of time, determined by the children and during which they all long to be near the lucky one. Luckier still is the child who spots an airplane, but it does happen. Once every couple months, an ole wild hare aviator out of Mosestown gets a prop turning on heeyoochul, and sputters over a ridge and out of sight, and the children run with their eyes on the sky, making sounds they didn't know they could. Then they sit in a circle and argue endlessly about whether every steel drum of jet fuel got burned up or not.

I tell them, "Children, don't miss the forest for the trees. There's no need for fuel when your compass is a magnet." It's been nine years since the last of the big burns and buybacks, and domestic planes were grounded by then anyway, avionic satellites floating dead, radio towers taken out quick as they were built. The children need to know what broke in order to build a better way. Until then, it is what it is, and you ain't getting off the ground in no iron bird, no matter how many times your pilot taps the glass.

There are traveling talepackers who stop at the trading post every now and again, and they all spin the story of the Bygone Pilot. A couple of them call it *Aviator No More*. These are buskined affairs with theatrical face contortions and two props—headphones and aviator sunglasses. There's always a whole lot of pleading hand gestures reminiscent of a Punch and Judy show. It's the tale of old men and women who seek out the airplane graveyard and climb their stepladder and mount the cockpit, and there they sit and deliver a monologue, tapping those little invisible glass circles for hours, waiting for the needle to jump. It never jumps. That's the money line every time. *It never jumps.* They remove their sunglasses and wipe at trained tears. "I wanna fly again," they plead. "Please, God, let me fly again." The talepackers are spinning memories of movies. It's a tired affair.

Heeyoochul is what the real aviators in Mosestown call their home-made fuel. It's hooch fuel. I knew an old woman who sipped it one time.

I was fond of the floatplane, for I once grew fat and rich and trav-eled to islands by floatplane, and on these islands I slept in white hotels with blue dome roofs where guestbooks were filled with the complaints of former guests. They wrote: *Why must the insects be so loud? Something must be done about the incessant call of the insects and the birds, who are relentless.* And so something was done. The hotels had consolidated their management and a decision was made to spray pesticides and to leave upon windowsills crumbs of poisoned bread. And do you know that it worked? The islands grew silent except for the buzz of the mopeds.

No matter, for the children of the wealthy traveler had grown weary of being outdoors. There was too much that was soiled and infectious. There were startling sights and sounds that might damage the sensitive children. The outdoors were so different from the call of their tablets, to which they had become accustomed. Once, in the belly of a Cessna, I broke a tablet over my knee, but that is a story for another time.

My littlest grandbabies weren't yet born in the time of the wealthy traveler who complained in the hotel guestbook. They hear of it from the older children and they can't imagine such a time and place. They come to me and ask for a song. I let the little ones climb my legs and get on my lap. They love to lay their heavy heads on me and I am happy for the weight. I tell them: "The traveler could fly over an ocean in the stomach of an iron bird while their children cried or stared at a square of glass in their lap, window shade drawn while the earth rolled below, map of everything. There was jet fuel making it all happen. There were bags of crackers shaped like fish and innumerable bottles of water. The wealthy traveler ate the fish and drank the water and left the trash where they felt like leaving it. And the tired ones walked the aisle with a bag, asking for the trash. And the rich ones walked the same aisle to the tiny restroom, where they peed in a hole and pressed a button."

About half of the children ask only about the screen: "What was on the square of glass, BigMom? Was it cartoon animals speaking

Spanish? Was it outer space? Was it secret tunnels?" This really tickles me because I know why they ask such things, and I'll tell you. My nephew Rimmy Knox one time hooked a TV/VCR unit to a solar module he'd rigged on the pole barn roof, and it ran for three hours before it died with the tape still stuck inside. It was a bootleg tape: The first hour and forty-one minutes of *2001: A Space Odyssey*, followed by *Rikki-Tikki-Tavi*—dubbed en Español— followed by a single episode of *The Last Airbender*.

The children do a beautiful cover of a song from the tape. Some nights they use djembe, mandolin, and uke; some nights lute and pipa. We all breathe deep and roar on the final chorus, *Secret tunnel!* The children will talk about that tape forever. They'll get a little older and pass down the tale of the tape to the younger ones, and it will root up and bloom, and people will speak of the glowing robot screen—of monolith and mongoose, cobra and stars—and the tale of the tape will be in the blood, inherited the way people once inherited coal and caste and ceaseless trauma.

On Thursdays the children trade old photographs. They call it PictureSwap. There's three or four boys that don't even look at the people's faces. These boys have eyes only for the vehicle in the background. Magnifying glasses are produced. "It's a Cadillac! Look here." Other days they'll argue endlessly about whether or not every last bullet was really melted after the buyback in '29. Without fail, one of them always says they heard folks were making new bullets in a smelter, and that's when I tell them: "Children, don't miss the fire for the smoke. How you going to hide a blast furnace?"

The littlest ones love the time each evening just before fireside songs, when they go off with the older ones to look for secret tunnels and pick blackbone from the crumbling high wall at Switch Rock. A coal seam runs horizontal there in one wide stripe, and they fill their buckets up with fallen chips and walk the footpath back in a line, and when they come to toss their catch in the big pit, I look at them, waiting on the fire shoulder to shoulder with their dirty buckets, laughing, and I am happy. Sometimes I cry because they look like the old photographs I've seen at PictureSwap, the shoulder-to-shoulder boys who always smiled when their picture was made because they'd stepped off the cage to live another day, empty dinner bucket hooked at the elbow, carbide lamp sagged on the brow, faces black no matter their tint, pickaxe snug as a hand on the shoulder. They had coal in their blood. They had cold beer waiting, and whiskey, and the temporary glee of having made it back up the shaft once again.

I was alive when the foreman said a mule was worth more than a man. Before that time, it was the other way around and, later, it would be so again. I'm still waiting on the day when *worth* sees its end, a day when we can start to begin. Maybe it'll be tomorrow. I surely know it wasn't yesterday.

Only thing I can remember some days is how to forget. I forget what these scars mean on the softwood arm of my highback captain's chair. *12.25.38*. I counted up seventeen *12.25.38*s just this morning. And along the arm's slick maple edge: turnbuck , seventeen of those too. I don't recall carving them, but what can you do? It is our blood that remembers anyway, our blood that carries everything. Your blood is mine and mine is yours. You stick your tongue between your front teeth when you concentrate because your great-great-great-great-grandmother stuck her tongue between her front teeth when she pinned a diaper or arm-wrestled a woodhick or wrote a letter to her cousin or cut a line in the dirt for dropping seeds.

I will write to you and I will sing for you too. I will do my best with what I have left. I don't rightly know myself what's a dream and what's awake anymore, but I will chase a pinhole of light to the end of every row, and if all goes dark, I'll turn around and find the light, and chase it down again.

I am a MuleBird and this is my song.

SONG OF THE WORKSHIRT

I made the WorkShirt I wear. Can you guess how many pockets I have sewn? It started with nine but now it has grown. Nine thousand pockets my shirt now boasts, and every one holds a fold of paper. There is nothing I like more than when a child reaches up and into a pocket, and pulls out a fold. Some wear fear as they do it, little hand shaking, eyes asking if it's okay to open. "Open it," I say. "Read what it says." And then, just like Auntie Eel, I tell them, "It's a fortune all for you." Other children snatch and unfold straightaway, no permission needed. I don't mind the method and I don't catalog the style. I only watch their little eyes move across what their little hands hold, and it never registers right away, what's written, and so I watch them read it again. And when they look up, before they can speak, I blow a gust of air in their little faces, and they sneeze, and the story on their fold of paper disappears. But I don't disappear. I remain.

Remaining is how I got my second name. I am the Everywhen Woman.

A girl in southern West Virginia said it first, more than three hundred years ago, before there was any such thing as West Virginia, back when the land still held its original people. She spoke another tongue when she said it. She was remarking on how I seemed to be everywhere all the time.

Meta'thenee Kweewa is what she called me. Or at least that's my best estimation of what she said. The first time she spoke it she was standing in knee-high water, fishing at a switchback on Sharp Creek. You should have seen the trout.

Her name was Ma se ki ke. I never could say it real well so she told me to call her Magnolia, her favorite English word. I called her my cousin sometimes, too, and I loved her the way I loved Aunt Ida and Georgie Smythe, and later on the Baaches of Keystone and the Knoxes of Mosestown. Of all the people I've loved, only Ida was blood kin. Magnolia was Shawnee and I was white, same as them who would come to kill her people and march her descendants to Kansas, but me and Magnolia came up on the same ground with only a hill between us. That hill marked the edge of Shawnee hunting grounds. I was eight years old when I first saw her by the beech tree on the banks of Sharp Creek. She was ten but smaller than me. We'd both been walking alone. I waved to her and she waved back.

Her people didn't like to stay put. But in the spring and summertime, we'd meet on Sharp Creek. We traded smooth rocks we'd painted pictures on. We traded knives. We traded words and the naming of things. This was before all the bloodletting and fire, before that man took her life and chalked my course.

It was nearly three hundred years after Magnolia died that I would come to see her in the eyes and hear her in the words of one of my grandbabies, a magnificent beautiful girl named Memphis Tennessee Knox, and this is why I believe in reincarnation, and why I believe in suffering.

The little ones call me BigMom. I don't call myself anything, and I don't mind what I'm called. You can call me PuddinTain. You can call me Betty.

If you are wondering how I can fit 9,000 pockets on my shirt, or how I have lived thrice as long as any other human animal, that is perfectly logical. I don't blame your disbelief, should that be how you feel. What can I say? I am an old fart and I just keep rumbling.

* * *

My nephew Rimmy Knox is a sculptor of magical scrapyard tele-graph machines, but he draws a little too. He has made twenty-two pictures all for you. Here is one he made of me in my favorite old hat with a little sprig of flowers, winking like I do.

The stitching is torn on my most-used pocket. The Don't Forget pocket, within easy reach. Don't forget to oil your rifle. Don't forget to make the donuts. Don't forget to pick up Memphis at work.

On a recent Tuesday, in order that I might shape my existence with some routine, I reached for a slip of paper in the Don't Forget pocket at my right armpit, and wouldn't you know there was no shirt there atall? No brassiere either. No pants, no underwear.

I was naked as a jaybird again.

SONG OF THE LLAMA

Once upon a time there lived a llama. And I hope you don't mind that his name was Larry because it really was. Not Lawrence shortened to Larry.

Just Larry. Larry from birth. Larry the llama.

Larry's parents, you see, were from Terre Haute, and they were big Larry Bird fans, and they'd always admired that Larry Joe Bird's parents had named him just that. No Lawrence, no Joseph. Nothing fancy. Nothing at all fancy.

Anyway, Larry the llama was always interrupting himself, mid-conversation, to quote a TV show he'd once loved, to call out his own long-windedness by way of saying, in a German accent, *Your story has grown tiresome!* He was very aware is what I'm telling you. He was nervous and he talked too much.

*   *   *

Mostly he did impressions of his favorite television and film characters. He did a nice James Bond, the Roger Moore variety. He did Serpico. He did a spot on *Barnaby Jones* and a solid Uncle June from *The Sopranos*. Larry was a talented, good llama. Loving. Generous. It's only that he was perpetually ahead of the game. A llama before his time. He got tired of the *your mama so fat* jokes real early on, and he could always see straight through a line of bull crap. He applied himself as a pack animal in the fields and on the hillsides, but at night, for months, he wandered to the same washed-out corner of the pasture, alone, and there, in 1999, he dug a trench and ran away from everyone he'd ever known.

He was two.

He got picked up on the side of State Route 58 east of Elnora by a couple in a Chevy S10 with one wide stripe. They sold him to a peculiar Englishman who owned a zoo back in Liverpool. That man shipped Larry to Liverpool, and a year later another man bought him and Larry eventually settled into a life of being touched and fed at a petting zoo in Newcastle upon Tyne before he was rescued and brought to live comfortably at a sanctuary in Longhorsely, Northumberland. There, one night, twenty years after he left Indiana, for no known reason, somebody shot and killed him.

I tell you this not to upset you or disturb your trust or sense of peace in reading. I tell you because I want you to be prepared. I want you to make it through what's coming. One part of a storyteller's duty is to offer up some truth. And the truth is that sometimes, in order to maintain the sanctity of the life of animals and trees and land and water, we must tell not only of their living times but of their death as well. For death is a part of life, and though it is a great hardship for the living to endure, endure it we must.

I will help you. I have a great deal of knowledge concerning the endurance of pain and sorrow. If I tell you of the life and death of the people I loved—of Magnolia and Memphis and Eel and Stan—it might help you make it through. It might help you and me both find the light.

One thing I've learned is that we ought not anticipate death all the live-long day. Those who await the end miss the middle. Those who dance naked on a porch roof at sunrise don't miss much at all.

Say what you will about Larry, but he did his thing.

I am a llama and you are too.

SONG OF THE NASCENT

I was born in 1717 in what some folks called the Colony of Virginia. In truth, it was Five Nations land. Of my ancestry, I know only that my mother Martha was a thin, milk-skinned seamstress from England. I had no daddy to speak of, and since my tint was darker than my mother's, some said my daddy was an itinerant elk hunter name of Earl, half Shawnee, but I came to know such talk as little more than a thing white people said when there wasn't any daddy to speak of. I came up white, and I saw that they'll kill you if you're otherwise. My mother never said one word on who my daddy was, but I've seen him walking in traffic, and I've seen him squatting on the hood of a Cadillac. I once saw him climbing a lamppost in Sevilla at four in the morning. He looked all around, climbed the iron pole, licked his thumb, and opened the little glass door by the trickling flame. From inside he plucked a foil-wrapped brick of hashish, broke off a couple of grams, and sold it to the man I was trailing. Later, when I picked that man clean, I smoked his hash and communed with the dead and ate canned fish while stars rode the ripples of the Guadalquivir.

I was born on the third day of March, in a cellar. Those present were my mother's two sisters, Jane and Ida, who delivered me. Above us, there roared a great winter blizzard that took from us those loved ones who had not found shelter. I grew up hearing of that all-powerful snowstorm, the kind none would see again until 1888, and then again in 2023.

When I was four I climbed to the highest branch of a shagbark hickory out back of our home. The branch broke, and I fell forty feet or more to the hard ground below. My Aunt Ida was the only one to witness. She screamed and gathered me up and held me to her chest and cried and cried. When I began to breathe, she found herself unable to. When I opened my eyes and hugged her back, she wondered if her life had become a dream. She swore that any human animal would die from such a fall, but after I hugged her a while, I stood, and dusted my trousers, and looked up at the tree's canopy and climbed it again.

I suppose I might have known then that I could not die an earthly death, but I was yet too young to know such a thing. I would not understand it for certain until I was seventeen, at the edge of a circle of light cast by a head-high fire, a pair of hands around my throat.

I have no explanation for my inability to die. I cannot tell you why, for the last 250 years, I have looked to be about seventy.

I can tell you it's very painful to live on while the ones you love are dying. This is particularly true in the case of the family I've lived with and loved for the last seventy years, the Knoxes of Mosestown. They have had more than their share of dying.

Like me, Stanley Knox fell from the high limb of a tree when he was four years old. It was 1979. A big sycamore in the backyard corner of the Knox's 9th Avenue home. I was the only one to witness. I screamed and gathered him up and held him to my chest and cried and cried. When he began to breathe, I opened my eyes and hugged him. I wondered if my life had become a dream. Little Stanley dusted himself off and climbed the tree again, and it was on that very day that I gave him his first nickname. In an ill-advised move, he would later tattoo it across his knuckles.

I write to you from Freon Hill, in the Great Free State of McDowell, where Black and brown and white and in-between have lived and loved together like this for a long time. Our particular acreage of

hill plateau was likely lived on first by the Adena people and, later, the Mingo. It was purchased by a white family named Hood in 1789. Stanley came into its possession in 2018 as a place to expand his cannabis crop. Most of us moved here full time between '23 and '25. That's when people started calling it Buckwheat Mountain. Sometimes, I'd just as soon not call it anything at all.

It's cold again but we have blankets. Out past the far ridge, there is still bad luck and trouble. For that, we have lookout towers, eight of them.

At the river barge docks and on Route 52, the scavengers congregate and get up to no good. The lingering white nationalists jabber and plan, a Turnbuck or two among them. We're ready for them if they come again. I was ready at four when I fell from the tree. I was ready at seventeen.

I am ready now, at 321.

SONG OF THE ROBOT

There was a song that my grandbabies used to love, a song that we would sing along to in the car on trips to the public pool. This was about halfway through President Obama's first term and we hadn't yet sniffed what was to come after him. I liked that time, the first half of 2010. Memphis Knox was our van's permanent DJ, and she favored a song called "Robots." Its chorus was *Robots need love too, they want to be loved by you.* The children sang it from the back of the van. It was August. Air conditioner broken and we were seven deep, headed to the pool again, dropping Memphis at work on the way. We were singing loud and the hot wind bent back our eyelashes and, for a moment, we were happy whether we knew it or not. When the song was over, my grandson asked me, "Is that true, BigMom?"

Is what true?

And then a coal truck had his treads on the middle yellow line, oncoming in a tight stretch with broken-down shoulders by the creek, and my job was to keep those children in back alive and so I couldn't give my full attention to their questions about robot love, for even though two of my nephews had hauled coal for Pittston and I've got nothing against a man who hauls rock or coal for his bread, when a fifty-ton Mack truck came fully over that yellow line and I had those children in the vehicle, I saw red. In my visions, I whipped the wheel and fishtailed a 180, ran him down, and plucked him by the neck from his seat. I told him what I knew about life and steel and death. He looked up at me from the blacktop, trying to get his wind back. He cried.

* * *

The child clarified his question about truth. "Is it true that robots need love too?"

No. It most certainly is not true. Don't be taken in, no matter what. When all is said and done, it will be clear. Robots are machines. We built machines once upon a time to move things and have been at it ever since. We begot the robots to move a multitude of things, even information, and after a while, every- thing we begot was a robot. And this was okay by most so long as the robot got the mule's job and the mule could presumably just walk around all day, chewing on things she found on the ground, certainly not straining so hard as to destroy her ligaments. But we allowed the robots to take the jobs of the people and then we put the robots all around us and we were sure to keep them in our pocket. They began to keep us entertained and informed, everywhere and always. They directed the movements of our fuel and our water and our wars. They directed the movements of our memories and imaginations. They carry out our learning and guide our future paths. The robots keep us alive even as they kill us.

I said some approximation of this to the children, although I said it without the benefit of hindsight. Do not misunderstand me. I am not a seer. There were plenty others singing that same tune about robots back then. The only true seer I knew was Stanley Knox and, at that time, he'd not yet found his vision. In August 2010, Stan was drunk on penitentiary wine, five months left on his sentence.

That van's suspension rolled like a waterbed, I'll tell you what. I steered round potholes the size of paint cans.

I know for certain it was August 20. We were dropping Memphis off at work, a headshop/adult toy emporium on Beechnut Street.

It was called Sunshine&Ice. Inside, there were dildos and water-bongs everywhere, tilted just so in their clear acrylic display stands.

At the intersection of Grapevine and 12th Street, an itinerant man in silver NASA pajamas walked out in front of the moving convertible ahead of us. The brakes were up to date and the tires filled to perfect psi so as to keep the rubber squeal relatively quiet. No horn sounded. Everybody lived. The man in the NASA paja-mas wore day-old face paint, white and cracked at the chin. He unhooked his thumbs from the straps of his overstuffed backpack and waved two-handed to the convertible people. He took to the sidewalk, skipped right on by my open window. He was so very dirty and wore an Elks Lodge ball cap. He spun in a circle and blew me a kiss.

"Why do you have to say shit like that, BigMom?" Memphis was nineteen and always riding shotgun. Oh how I loved Memphis Knox. Of all the children I've known, she held the brightest light.

We pulled up to Sunshine&Ice. The concrete parking chocks were crumbling. I asked her to clarify, something I was always asking from the children back then. I said, "Why do I have to say shit like *what*, Memphis?"

"Shit like the robots kill us and keep us alive and all that." She looked me in the eyes and pointed at the kids. "They're too lit-tle," she said. Her hair was pulled back. Her eyes were tired and beautiful. She wore a new tattoo on the inside hinge of her right elbow: *the master of ceremonies to all forms of truth.*

I told Memphis I said shit like that to make them all *think* a little bit.

*   *   *

It was quiet in the back.

Memphis popped open the door to get out. "I've spent too many years trying *not* to think," she said. "I ain't about to start up again now."

We watched her go to the door, barefoot with her coffee in one hand, in the other her sandals and cigarette purse. She walked on the balls of her feet. Her linen shirt caught a gust of wind and held it. I'd made her the shirt as a gift for her sixteenth birthday. Hand-embroidered red-breasted nuthatches chased a needle and thread in a circle at the neckline. It was untucked and I can still see the white linen dancing in the hot wind. The whole storefront was black glass. Memphis pushed the white button and flipped the bird to the security camera. I drove off when they buzzed her in.

It was the last time I saw her.

Can you imagine that? Here was the last I would get of the little girl who'd been at my side since the time she could walk, dropping seeds in the vegetable garden, the little girl who frightened me when she was still in grade school. Meaning: such was the nature of her intelligence—it frightened you a little. Memphis was sharp as a boot spike, but her formative days were wildly unharbored. When she was born, her parents were sixteen, same age she was when I made her the linen shirt and told her my deepest truth.

On August 20, 2010, her daddy Stanley Knox was in prison and her mother Lissa Hornbuckle was on the run, and so it was that Memphis had naturally discovered her newfound dedication to never think at all. I don't know what her final words were in those hours to follow or to whom she spoke them, but the last words she spoke to me are ones I am meant to remember: *I've spent too many years trying* not *to think. I ain't about to start up again now.* I have often thought, before then and since, about whether we ought to *think* in this life, or whether instead we ought to just dance naked on a mountain at dawn all the live-long day, or whether life ought to be some circular pie percentage chart wherein if you get your clock punched and cripple your wrist pushing buttons or you stiff your back picking radish in hundred-degree heat, the least you might be afforded is to decide if you want to *think* about it all or not. I am not meant to know nor to judge what is right. We are, none of us, meant to know. What we are meant to do is never know, together, and without any fear.

I drove onward toward the pool. We passed a stand of spruce trees and one was broken open at the middle, laid over by the storm.

"Look, children!" I pointed out the window.
I called it out. "Splintercat!"

Back then, I was always reading to them from *Kickle Snifters and Other Fearsome Creatures.*

If we were lucky, we'd beat the bus from the Boys&Girls Club and get a good patch of grass on the pool's east end. But I felt the need to speak on some things to the children, and I needed to park the van in order to do so. I needed to turn around in my seat and look the children in the eyes.

I pulled off Brown Bag Road and drove up the hill. I rolled slow to the far corner of the giant lot at the dead Kmart. A blue dumpster had its lid thrown open and I swear a crow sat on each of the four corners, watching. The sheen on their wings was lit by the morning sun. Those crows glowed.

The six-year-old said, "This ain't the pool."

The baby had farted again and everyone put their t-shirts over their noses. I looked at the baby in the rearview. She smiled a knowing kind of smile. She pulled a stuck cheerio from the armrest of her car seat and ate it. I loved such moments more than I can put in words. It was a moment in the time of Memphis Knox among the living. To be alive in that time, in a wide hollow between two hills, with no one around but the glowing blackbirds, and then to see a smiling farting baby in a rear-facing mirror? I don't care if it's real or a dream. It is everything to me and it always will be so.

I put the van in park and turned around in my captain's chair to face them. I said to take their shirts off their faces and breathe deep the natural scents of this world. I said, "Were you children listening about the robots?"

"They kill us?" a big one said.

"Well, they don't only kill us. They do everything for and to us. And soon, we will clutch them in our hand instead of our coffee or our keys or shoes, and then, later on, some folks will put them inside their skin."

"The robots?"

"Yes."

* * *

"Who will?"

"Rich folks. And by then they will have taught themselves so intricately how to pretend to love but to truly hate a robot that it will be easy to likewise hate their fellow human animals, for what are we really, but labor force, with no upgrades or enhancements, and they won't need that anymore."

It was quiet. I knew I might be wrong about everything. I said as much to the children. I said, "Look here, children, I might be wrong about all this."

They were so very quiet. Quiet as the future hills of truant birds out beyond the dead Kmart. My ears commenced to ringing.

From up on the ridge, air brakes boomed like a jackhammer's echo.

I asked who wanted to go get a Dr. Pepper Slush. Everybody did.

I am not a robot and neither are you.

SONG OF THE TREE

Try to remember that a living tree is only half of the story. The other half is under the ground. Try to imagine that the roots reach wide as a house and deep as a well.

Every human animal has the silhouette of a tree burned somewhere inside. Close your eyes and see it. Mine is a great big beech tree shaped like somebody dropped a grenade at its middle and the little tree grew up around the crater, a hand with six fingers.

I am partial to primitive-style renderings of family trees. I'll offer here, for you, the inosculated family tree of the Knoxes of Mosestown. Short roots, grafted trunk, and gemel branches. These are the people who live inside my songs. They are one of my families, and I belong to them.

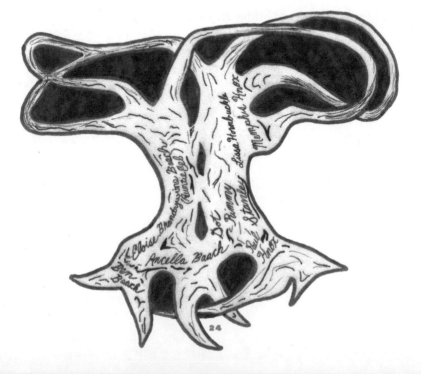

Trees rub against one another in the wind until the outer bark is gone, at which point they rub each other's inner parts until they grow one-into-the-other, until they are singular.

Aunt Jane's husband Homer was a McDowell County woodhick. He was from Switchback, an axe man and boom poke who walked across floating logs just as easy as an afternoon stroll. He said that if you had to take down trees for your bread, you'd better plant as many as you drop. I don't think that notion caught on with his contemporaries. Homer died when I was five, on a Sunday, on the water. He was in the log dump. His caulk boot caught a knot and he was yanked down in a hard roll, knocked unconscious when his head smacked the timber. He slid limp into a black gap of water that clacked shut just as dull and quick as it had opened. Homer was too soft for the life of a knot bumper. Trees will always make widows.

Close your eyes, knot bumper, and know the layer you take! That was the last thing Magnolia said. I can see her still, clear as a picture hung on the wall, standing in black of night next to the head-high fire, creek beyond catching light from the moon, everybody wild drunk on hooch.

She screamed it at him, the white man who'd told her he loved her. He'd been in the bottle for four days. He was so tall next to her, shirtless and slicked with sweat, mumbling about taking down every tree for a hundred miles. His forearms were thick. His fingers curled like talons. The whites of his eyes weren't white at all.

Magnolia could hardly stand. She was slight of build and had slugged five times or more from the long brown bottle. She'd not said a word for an hour when all at once, in clear English, she pointed her finger up at his face and screamed it. "Close your eyes, knot bumper, and know the layer you take!"

He killed her. The moment she spoke it on the air, he grabbed her by the hair with his left hand, knocked her out cold with his right, and threw her in the fire like a rag doll. I couldn't get her out. I ran up on the pit but he caught me by the coat and kept me back. Oh, how I screamed, enough to ring my own ears. He tried to kill me next but he couldn't. He put me to the ground hard and sat on my chest and choked my throat with all that he had and still I lived. He bore down harder. The backs of my pupils detonated a thousand radiant moons and filled my skull with pinholes of light but still I lived. Bolts of fire issued from my limbs and I saw an endless helix of dark darting strokes, but the light came back and with it, this world. That's the night I understood I couldn't die an earthly death. He understood it, too, and the fear it put in his eyes was the most powerful kind of fear you're liable to ever see. His hands gave out and he backed away quick. I ran into the woods and hid. I cried and cried.

Since that night, whether dark early morning or daylight nap, I have had ninety-nine recurring dreams, cycled like clockwork beneath my time, only the faces and voices changing as the faces and voices of my waking life change. I began logging the dreams a couple of years in, numbering them in a thread-bound book of rag paper, and when that was filled, straw paper, and after that wood pulp, and later on storebought paper, staple-bound.

Somewhere close by, in every last one of those dreams, were always that man's choking hands.

* * *

His initials were carved on tree trunks and branded on butt cuts all across the colony in the old old days. I can see those initials still. Scar on the rind, burn at the middle: *S. W.*

After he killed Magnolia, seven months passed, and then, on a Monday morning in May before the sun came up, I took five apples from my sack and fed the five tied horses I'd tracked. We were inside a circle of red spruce. I left them each a fistful of sugarcubes and whispered shhh shhh shhh shhh. I crawled from the circle and crouched next to S.W. where he slept on the ground. Four men I'd never seen slept alongside him. Corn liquor heavy on the air, no wind. The smoke from the pit was weak and thin. I straddled the saddlebag he'd fashioned as a pillow. I took out a once-used straight blade for which I'd traded the barber a stag-handled hunting knife, and on that early May morning, I pulled the straight blade under the sleeping man's jaw and left a note pinned to his breast pocket that read: *I am ready for all of you men, have always been ready, and if you harm my sisters, so I harm you, and if you take their life, so I will take yours.*

I have found this method to be very effective over the years in sending a clear message.

I am a tree and so are you.

SONG OF THE EXALTED

A woman like me didn't once upon a time get rich and fat for no good reason. I'm still fat, but I wasn't ever rich, save for the year 2020. Then I lost my mind, again. On an airplane, again.

The first time I lost my mind on an airplane was the first time I flew in one. It was Super Bowl Sunday, January 12, 1975, and my dear friend Carroll Wilson had bought us the tickets to Brussels. She'd plied me with Tennessee whiskey and a big white pill she called Velveteen. I fell asleep before takeoff, woke up over the English Channel, stepped into the aisle, lowered my underwear, squatted, and made water, right there at the armrest of the bald-headed gentleman reading his London *Times*. He called me Miss, asked if I was all right. I said, "Good Lord, these wax figurines can move and talk?" That's when the flatulence commenced, and then I ran headlong toward the cockpit, for I was convinced it was the public toilet, the one in the basement labyrinth of what I knew my current location to be: the International Museum of Wax Figured Humans in Church Pews. The IMWFHCP.

The second time I lost my mind on an airplane was the last time I flew in one. It was March 3, 2020, my birthday, about a month before Covid put a halt to such travel. I was on a float plane from Elefsina to Mykonos. I'd been flying all over the world for eighteen months at that point, having cultivated an international following for *FCGR*, the little book I'd written, but on this day, inside this particular airplane, I heard my own voice calling out to me, and it said: *This is a beautiful country! I have not cast my eyes over it before!* and I looked over the headrest of the child in front of me and watched him watch his tablet, and wouldn't you know he'd pulled up the infamous video of August 3, 2017, the one that got my exalted engine cranking, the one that got 13 million views on YouTube and brought bad luck and trouble back to Stanley, and chalked our course, once again, with the Turnbucks.

The littlest children don't know what YouTube was, and that tickles me. One time I mentioned it at storytime and the youngest child said, "Was that yogurt in a pouch?" I said, "No, sweetbaby, that was moo-tubes."

It was just too much, seeing that boy watch another me on his screen. Here I was, my book tour publicist at my side with a stack of *FCGR*s for me to sign before our next speaking engagement, an exclusive retreat for rich philanthropists who fancied themselves revolutionaries, another in a line of sell-out events masquerading as resistance. I was drinking Bombay gin in the belly of an iron bird while a small rich child watched the other me, the one from three years prior, the one with a red bandana around her throat and a sign in her fist: *Hillbillies Against trump.* In the video, my feet are planted on stacked flowerbed pavers out front of the Mosestown Civic Center, where, inside, little donnie trump jabbered and gibbered and spluttered and muffled. A crowd of a hundred or so fellow protesters stood before me. In my other fist, a bullhorn. I called to them, full-throated:

"Oh, the dread of he who can balbuciate hate. Go back to Palm Beach, Captain Clusterfuck! West Virginia don't want you here!"

They let out a relatively mighty roar.

I called the words of Lucy Parsons. "Oh, starved, outraged, and robbed laborer," I pleaded, "how long will you lend attentive ear to the authors of your misery?"

*   *   *

My nephews Stanley and Rimmy, my niece Dot, all can be seen handing out my little staple-bound pamphlet to the crowd. Cost me two hundred bones to copy enough for that day. *The Fortify Collective Guide to Resistance.* The *FCGR*, as it came to be known. Back then, it was printed local by Barbara Ailes's print shop. I couldn't conceive of its rapid spread or worldwide reach, nor my subsequent lucrative publishing contracts in seventeen languages, nor the pamphlet's evolution from a humble black-and-white staple-bound thing to a hard-spined, full-color, coffee-table kind of life.

And here was the wealthy child, with his fingers caked in the residue of the yellow fish cracker, a pile of trash at his feet. I knew the couple beside him were his parents, on their way to hear me speak on anarchic socialism in the ballroom of an exclusive Greek resort, $1,200 a plate. I knew his eyes, as he watched, were dead, his ears stuffed with crumbs of bread. In the video, under shadow of the Civic Center's marquee, I spoke dire warnings of racist fascism. I called forth revolutionaries. A young woman had filmed it all from her perch upon the abstract aluminum sculpture at plaza's middle. What she captured next would prove key to the video's spread, and key to all the rest of it too.

A wiry trumpist in a white t-shirt cursed me as he pushed through the crowd. "You shut your goddamned mouth!" he screamed, again and again. I saw him coming all the way. Red-hat, red-face, spittle-spewing, shit-boned devil. It was only when he got to me that I recognized his eyes. He was a Turnbuck boy. He grabbed the hem of my blue jeans and yanked. He was stronger than he looked. Nearly took me down from my perch. I wobbled but did not fall. There was a collective gasp of disapproval. They saw me as elderly, vulnerable. They did not know of my revenge-driven propensity to violence, nor my instinct to kick the man in the eye socket with my steel-toe Chippewa.

* * *

I did not want to kick the man in the eye socket that day, for there were children present, and I was trying to get shed of the violence, and help them make a better way. So I didn't kick him, and he yanked my hem again, hard, and I went down on my tailbone in the planter.

Stanley shot from the denizens like a serpent's strike, his remaining pamphlets scattered on the wind, his cocked fist exploding against the man's cheekbone with a crack that seemed to find its way through my bullhorn.

The groans from the crowd were discernible and operatic. A couple of folks cheered. The wiry trumpist lay prone, his middle rising and falling and rising and falling.

A skinny shirtless boy came forth and stood over him, and expertly hollered a line from the oft-quoted film: "You got knocked the fuck out!"

I shan't go on about the rest of the video at this juncture. I did not allow it to proceed any further that day in the floatplane. The twin engines roared like a fire in my ears. I undid my safety belt and knocked back the end of my gin. Something was rising inside me.

My publicist looked at me and said, "You really shouldn't unfasten your seatbelt." She tapped the stack of books as I stood. "And you've got twenty more books to sign."

"Shut up, Gertrude," I said, and then I took a step forward and reached down and jerked the child's tablet from his greasy dusted fingers.

* * *

"Hey!" he said. I did not care for his pronunciation. I mocked it and sent it back to him, elongating the middle and slumping my shoulders and making my face as ugly as I could. His parents turned away from their phones in unison and regarded me with a wonderful combination of recognition and disgust.

I jutted my neck their way and changed my facial expression in an instant. I went bug-eyed and they recoiled. I used my practiced tongue and lips to call a long wet fart slapple.

I raised up the tablet and held it flat like a silver serving tray. I cocked my knee. The whoosh from my downswing/upstroke whipped the fine forehead hairs of the wealthy child and he flinched just before his lip curled to cry.

The tablet had made a pleasingly textural crunch as it tentpoled across my thigh.

I walked to the little brass cabinetry knob where the black plastic trash bag hung. The flight attendant sat at attention, her mouth agape. I winked at her and chucked the smashed tablet in the bag and watched the edges tear through, a slow-motion triangle.

When I passed the child on the way to my seat, I bent to him so close I could smell the salt in his tears. I noted the goldenbrown hue of his eyes. I whispered, "You're a lucky little boy. I might have opened the plane's side door to toss away your foul toy, but then we'd all have been sucked to our deaths upon the wind, wouldn't we?"

And he quit his crying, and nodded his head, and knew himself to be lucky. He knew—I could see in his eyes—that I'd bestowed on him a gift.

*   *   *

His parents did not see it that way. They cried foul and allowed their hatred to leak out. They demanded to know what kind of person did such a thing.

I said: "Well, you were fixing to come hear me speak."

We hit a turbulent patch and the child shrieked like a wildcat and suddenly I was off the ground and my head hit the ceiling before I landed softly on my feet again.

The flight attendant ordered me to my seat. The child's father continued our conversation as if I'd not just floated to the ceiling. "We wouldn't have paid to hear you speak if we'd known you were such a fat bitch."

I smiled at him. Winked. Blew him a kiss and then told him if he wanted to, he could fuck around and find out.

Gertrude had set about sobbing.

My ears had set about ringing, loud as a theremin. I'd gone to the bad place again.

They let me deplane with dignity. Then a tall uniformed man with an extravagant mustache slapped on the cuffs and I marched the march I'd made so many times before. Ah, the choky.

Greek choky is good choky. An old woman with John L. Lewis eyebrows slipped me a rag-wrapped present through the painted bars. I pulled the tidy knot of twine. Inside was a baby food jar, three-quarters full of ouzo.

I managed to catch a ride back to the states on a giant tramp-tanker carrying olive oil and god knew what else. The captain was a kind and beautiful man who had read my book, said he was a fan and that my writing reminded him of Studs Terkel. Said every living thing was free as a falcon, paraphrasing a passage I'd written. He had me sign his copy of the *FCGR* like so: *For Cap. Take it easy, but take it*. He was the one who paid my bail.

I believe I may have told that man I loved him, but that is a story for another time.

I am a jailbird and my tendency to reoffend is legendary.

SONG OF THE RECIDIVIST

One time, in 1967, I spent a couple of days in the choky at Matewan, West Virginia, after a handsome troubled boy I knew had gone to six showings of *Cool Hand Luke* at the theater in Huntington, and then got drunk on Thunderbird—good and cold—and cut the heads off a row of parking meters on 4th Avenue. He drove out of there before they knew who'd done it, but the Huntington PD got a tip on the red '64 Corvair he'd driven away, and they trailed him across three counties, all the way to Red Jacket, where they gave close chase, and he ditched the car beside a shut-down tipple and ran for the hills. I was out on a walk and saw it all. When the officers stepped from their vehicle and said they were chasing a man who'd cut the heads off nine parking meters, I told them it was me who'd done it.

"It was *you?*" the smart one said, his brows up, his capacity to believe stretched.

"That's right."

"All right, then. What tool did you use to do it?"

I said, "Pipe cutter, Nye number 3, heavy duty."

About that time, the dumbest man in the world pulled up in his cruiser with a cracked cone headlamp. Ole Busy Bill Workman, sheriff's office dimwit.

He dismounted slow and old and said, "I'll take her from here, boys. She's a regular at the drinker clinker." The exhaust from his vehicle was dark on the air. He wiped at his long nose with a lavender handkerchief.

"Hey, Busy Bill," I said.

"Hey, Betty." He blushed, his squinted eyes tearing up like usual. Busy Bill was always leaking from the eyes and nose, and it was impossible to tell when he was crying and when he wasn't. He was a known crier, the kind who could always play it off and blame it on coal dust.

He'd been sweet on me for ten years by then, and so I went to the choky at Matewan and sat and talked to him for twenty-four hours from behind bars, but this was one of those weird times where I'd begun to spot again, sometimes getting a full-on period despite the fact that I was 250 years of age, and so I said: "Say hey, Busy, I reckon I need you to run to the store and pick me up some Kotex."

And Busy Bill said, "Now you know I love you, sweetie, but when you're in this here jail, you'll eat what everybody else eats."

And I laughed so hard I nearly cried. That dumbshit thought Kotex was a culinary request.

I once was lost. I never was found.

SONG OF MEMORY

Here is a thing I'll never forget: the time I saw Stanley Knox's brain on a stainless-steel tray in the fluorescent room of the skinny mortician. It was a big and glistening thing. I felt it pull on me. The black of its folds whispered quiet promises about suns you could hold in your hand. The folds were rivers, same as the dogleg cuts I'd seen from the windows of airplanes. And I knew then that the earth might be a brain, and that Stanley's brain was most certainly an earth. Once it had hummed electric but now the power was out. The whispers ended.

I believe the mortician may have said it was the heaviest brain he'd ever put on a scale.

That may not be so. I don't remember things right, as I told you before. I don't remember at all, most days. Time and memory braid up like hanks of hair. The longer the braid, the tighter the helix. The stems rot, the root dries, the serpent sheds its sheath.

I recall hanks of years and have no memory of other hanks. 1725 I remember. 1728. 1734 to 1751 I can picture and smell and taste. Then nothing. 1768 I know because that's when I first delivered a baby and fired a flintlock pistol. I remember 1774. 1777. 1855. 1860. 1888. 1912. 1948. 1967 to 1970. 2008. 2010. I remember 2017 to 2023 clear as crystal. 2029. I remember 2033.

I used to talk about memory, the importance of the past, but now I don't know what that means. Since I was very young I've had to wonder what is memory and what is imagination. I know one thing for certain: History, like they teach us in school, wasn't ever the real story. Take my most beloved city, Mosestown. They teach

the kids in school that their city is named for Hollis P. Moses, he
who made our railroads transcontinental and our coal worldwide.
He, the least known of the big five, those men who became wildly
rich on the returns from their railways and shipyards and coal piers.
Hollis Moses was born a farmer in Connecticut in 1818, and he
died a millionaire in New York City in 1910. Along the way, he
financed a boxcar foundry, four sawmills, two steel factories, and
a college, all of them inside a ten-mile strip of the West Virginia
river town that would come to bear his name.

To hell with Hollis P. Moses, I used to tell the children. Look
around you right now, I'd say. This is living history. This is your
city. Anybody you know rub shoulders with the Hollis Moses
caste? Where's that coal pier? Where's that factory? I told them
in the trump years most especially, because there never was any
such thing as trump country and there never will be. Our people
aren't who they say we are. In Mosestown, we were white and Black
and brown and Protestant and Catholic and Jew and Muslim and
Theravada Buddhist too. We are free as falcons. We are iron-willed
and peculiar in ways they'll never know. We grind the long game
because that's the only station we get out here. Remember that
about us.

If you're interested in memory, you ought to write down your
dreams. You have to try and remember dreams in this life. And
music. Music may be the best way to go about remembering. It
could be the fireside jam of the children. It could be Sam Cooke.
It could be the sound a knifeblade makes when it beheads a bean
and strings it clean. These days, I find myself humming the tune
to the old song "Bless the Telephone." Do you remember it? *It's
nice to hear your voice again.*

It's the song Stanley was listening to on the day of the total solar
eclipse. August 21, 2017, a Monday morning at Dot's big loft. That

day marked seven years since Memphis died. Stan was in a bad way. He'd not left his apartment in a week, after what had happened in Charlottesville. He'd already retreated after having knocked out the trumpist just a couple of weeks before. It turned out the trumpist was Peanut Turnbuck, younger brother of Pinch. Pinch had gone missing on Thanksgiving several years prior, and now Peanut had too. He'd suffered a concussion from Stan's punch but pressed no charges. When the video went viral, Peanut set out on a bender and ran off where not even his daddy could find him. His daddy was Chit Turnbuck, a racist cop in Huntington who'd been a senior at HHS in 1989 when Stanley, a freshman at MHS, rose up over him and dropped eight threes in his face at the state finals in Charleston. Chit Turnbuck had a special brand of hatred for white boys with a little bit of Black in them. He'd been after Stan so long we couldn't remember a time he wasn't.

Dot's Mosestown apartment was just what we all needed. There are days when I'd give up a finger just to dwell in an abode such as that again. One thing I loved about it was how the warehouse windows carried the morning sun in straight slashes. It was holy to behold. Stan had climbed on top of the freight elevator and ridden up that way, jumping off before the car quit moving. We cringed and hoped he'd not decapitate himself. We watched from the kitchen, where Dot was hand-cranking expensive coffee beans. The smell was uplifting. Wide hot beams lined the long floor, where cat-fur tumbleweeds drifted on the elevator's blast of air. Seven cats called Dot's place home, for if ever there was an alley cat she didn't refer to as "charismatic," I never made their acquaintance.

Fat Lever, the big Calico named for Dot's all-time favorite two-way guard Mr. Lafayette Lever, lay prone on the floor in the middle of a sunbeam. He'd killed two mice before 6 a.m. Slow deaths, both. Ample punctures, severed vertebra of the lower quadrant, each mouse flung high into the dusty air for good measure before expiring quietly along the bathroom baseboard.

It was rest time. Fat Lever quit licking his own frank&beans long enough to stare down Stanley, who stood in a sunbeam and stared right back until Fat had had just about enough. His back fluttered and flexed and, suddenly, he was flipped onto all fours and ready to launch.

Stanley just acted like he didn't give a flat damn about Fat, and the trouble diffused. Stan situated his parts and snorted and then took out his pocketknife to pare his nails. Fat walked over to the prefab bookshelf and jumped into an empty square.

The teakettle whistled and Dot did four things at once with a cigarette betwixt her long fingers, dragging on it now and again, ashing here and there in the flowerpots, blooming and steeping the grinds and feeding tuna fish to the cats spinning at her ankles. She called out to Stanley, "Mornin, baby brother. Coffee's four minutes from home."

So many of the Mosestown and Keystone women I've known moved in this way, talked in this way. They knew how to blow back smoke with their eyelashes, and the sound in their voice was perpetually low and sweet and settling, all the way up to the crack of doom.

Stan was taking a moment to himself after jumping off the elevator and confronting the feline flesh eater. He believed in powerful sevens, and he was having a hard time with this particular August's seven-year mark. I watched him inside the dusty beam, his black beard the shadow of a life-sized Punch&Judy chin. He wore his flip flops and yellow football socks, his LawnsByKnox hat. The old walkman hung on the waistband of his gym shorts, doing its job, for better or for worse. He swayed to the music with his head bowed. I walked over to where he stood. I heard the guitar chords when he dropped the headphones around his neck. Stan was crying. He pulled me to him tight and we hugged for a long time, the song coming quiet and loud from the little round earspeaker pinched between us: *I'm very much in love with you.*

You have to try and remember a morning like that one, no matter how troublesome. Remembering is merciful work.

The pockets on my WorkShirt came to be in this way. When the forgetting commenced in earnest, I began to write down my thoughts and memories and the things I needed to do, and I sewed the pockets on my shirt to house the notes. I wrote in empty matchbooks. I wrote in the margins of newspaper ads for honey-glazed ham. In one pocket, next to my bifocals, I kept a pair of miniature sewing scissors. In another, needle and thread. I stole golfers' pencils from the backs of church pews and dropped them into my little pockets so I'd never be without a tool. I kept them sharp with my jack knife, all the way down to the nub.

You can learn some things about the different denominations by staring deeply into the finish of their church pews. How much of the grain can you see? Are there any brushstrokes showing? Methodists like a lighter finish. Episcopalians, dark. Theravada Buddhists favor a golden shade. At the International Museum of Wax Figured Humans in Church Pews, I noted an in-between kind of hue.

Sometimes, when I stole the golfers' pencils, I'd fill out the church's guest card before I lit out, customarily at communion. The guest card questions were nearly identical across the denominations.

*   *   *

41

Welcome!

Date : __8-2-89__

Name : __Puddin__

Status: ☑ Single ☐ Married
tri-lingual, ready to mingle

Age Groups: ☑ 13-19 ☑ 20-29 ☑ 30-39 ☑ 40-49 ☑ 50-59 ☑ 60-Older

Children: *Wrench, Slim, Fat Girl, Tiny, Turtleneck, Stubby, etc.*

Where are you from?
Matewan by way of Naugatuck by way of Keystone

What brought you to our congregation? *D's*
Aint no stain glass at Captain D's

Is there anything else you'd like us to know about your family?
Junior will steal your last sugar cube and Aunt Sarry seasons her beans with skunk meat

It was always a whole lot of fun, writing in those church pew guest cards. Two or three times, I laughed heartily and loud as I wrote, right in there among the suit jackets and the girls who tied ribbons in their hair. They took me for a woman of the streets. I took them for what they were, and then I took my leave.

I never was much for church.

SONG OF SOLOMON WOOD

He ate what was handy and shat where he pleased. He sired children up and down every hollow. High Climber was where he got his start, way up in the big trees with a sharp-tooth saw and nary a rope to lash him. He smoked a clay pipe up there and looked out over the hogback ridges. He timed the thunderheads coming in from the west. For ten years, Solomon Wood drove timber down the Big Sandy River. "Let me see the spikes on them caulk boots," the other hill jacks would say, and they'd remark on the color of the studs. "Where you get these?" they'd ask, and Sol would light his pipe and swallow the match and say, "Any man rides his log knots up ought to fashion his own spikes from bone."

They were bobcat teeth, Sol's spikes.

He was the knot bumper whose throat I cut. He was the one who threw my cousin in the fire. That flash of shadow into light is branded on the backs of my eyes. It's a paint stroke, like the beech tree I see every time I blink.

I am the one come to make you remember the fire and the tree. The bone and the razor.

I am the one come to ask you the question: Have you ever truly thought of all the women, of all the girls, killed at the hands of a man? Have you conceived of such a figure as that? Such a vast and startling mountain of death? Conceive of it, and quiver.

I have fashioned a scythe from the jawbone of a doe. I have sharpened my cuspids with a wood rasp.

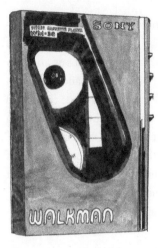

Here is Stanley's blue Sony walkman with a Dolby button. Fastforward broke a long time ago, so forget about skipping songs.

Rimmy Knox has a broken finger but he just keeps drawing right along.

Dot found the walkman in August inside a locked army storage trunk she hadn't had the nerve to open for fourteen years. The trunk belonged to Stanley. She said that one night, there was her nerve, restored once again. She gave the walkman to me, said she didn't want it, that nerve could only carry her so far. I noted Stanley's handwriting on the cassette tape inside: *Orchestrating Our Lives Volume 22.* I made a trade with Rimmy: my Hohner Marine Band for two AA batteries that he'd miraculously rejuiced. I thanked him, went to my cabin, sat on the mattress, and tucked the batteries into their beds. I put the headphones over my ears. The orange foam ear pads were moth-bit and rotten. The black rubber cord was cracked wide open. I rolled the volume wheel all the way to 10. I pressed the button.

The opening chord of "Bless the Telephone" by Labi Siffre surged through me from my belly to my brain and I was hugging Stanley Knox again where he stood by the freight elevator in his flip flops and yellow football socks, his deerstalker hat, his golden lens safety glasses. I could smell him.

* * *

Imagination is like memory, only stronger. It is equal parts mercy and hurt. It is a time machine. It runs, most efficiently, on mix tapes and psilocybin mushrooms.

The song ended. I backed it up and ran it again, and back and again after that. The batteries died. I cried. For Memphis, and for Stan, and for Stan's parents, Ancella and Paul, because I'll tell you something, and maybe you already know it, but I sure hope you don't. Sometimes in this life, there is nothing to be done. Paulie and Ancella lost their youngest boy who had himself lost his only girl. What of the suffering of the parent whose child dies? Gone at forty-nine, gone at nineteen. There is nothing that can be said or sung, written or called out in the empty night. There is nothing for this.

When the batteries died, I went outside, and I looked up at the moon, who cooled the surge and reminded me once again that I am very little. My time here—even my relatively extended time—is very very little.

I took off my clothes out there under the moon. I oscillated slow and regular to the crickets and katydids and the steady precise chorus in my ears, hand drums and theremin. A thousand goat-hide heads. Undulating jubilation howls.

The grass was wet and the ground under it was soft as dough, and down the hill, by the light of the moon, an old black walnut tree pulled its own roots from the earth. Two distinct legs rose up and stepped across the pitched hill. Dirt clumps hung by thin roots and swung, nightcrawlers writhing.

The tree faced me up from ten yards off. I tilted my head to crack my neck. The tree did the same. I did three jumping jacks and so did the tree. I danced, and it matched me, step for step. When I did the Mary-Poppins-Dick-Van-Dyke, the tree did the

Mary-Poppins-Dick-Van-Dyke. When I did the Shorty George, the tree did the Shorty George. Milly Rockin. Spank the Baby, now Magic Mike.

I waved goodbye and the tree waved back.

I was really tickled by that old black walnut. I laughed so hard I peed a little bit. The tree, so far as I could tell in the dark, did not pee. She turned and walked into the woods.

I turned and walked into my open door. I snatched my blanket from the bed and lay down on the floor. I fell fast asleep and dreamed recurring dream #88, the dream of the flying man who wore no face. He wore only a smear where his head should have been, until March of 2020, when the flying man of recurring dream #88 wore a singular face. It was the face of the little rich boy on the plane, his ever-trembling lip. In the dream, the boy soars overhead in maroon pajamas. He waves to me, like a tree might wave

I awoke early with that lucky old sun, and I climbed the ladder to my little porch roof, and I took down the lawn chair from its stovepipe nail, and unfolded it, and sat down naked facing east. One of my favorite inventions is most assuredly the folding chair.

Dot and Rimmy built the porch roof for me after I'd put the footers in the ground. I tell you what, I'm a shadow of the posthole digger I once was. But I went eight feet. If the big storm came back with hundred-degree wind, she could take my shack of matchsticks, but I'd chain my folding chair to the porch roof and stare her right in the eye.

Mostly I'd just wanted a good flat east-facing porch roof so I could sit and read in the morning sun, just like I'd wanted a good flat west-facing porch roof on which to dance naked. You can always switch back on which activity belongs on which roof. In any case, I needed those footers sunk deep, and I overworked myself, and got dehydrated, and down in that deep earth, I swear I saw rusted steel columns and a web of rebar, like we were sitting on ruins, and in the armpit of a soldered copper joint, I saw a glowing golden nest of some kind, like a water balloon filled with earthworms and motor oil, yellow as the sun, thumping like a heart.

Dot and Rimmy made that roof from the upturned hull of a flatbottom boat. I liked the way it felt on my feet, slick as glass. Rimmy secured one of his scrapmetal sculptures up there with a new adhesive he'd brewed. He said it was stronger than liquid nails. The sculpture was functional, a telepathic-telegraph machine of sorts from which he ran a line of copper to a solar panel he'd rigged on the stovepipe, just above the chair nail.

I wrote in my dream book up there about recurring dream #88, and then I closed the cover and went to Rimmy's machine and tapped out code on its big brass key like he'd showed me, and worked my jaw side to side, and hummed and listened and hummed and listened and hummed. Come to me boy, I thought. Come here to me.

I am trying to rid the world of regret.

SONG OF THE STRINGBEAN

Stringing beans taught me sound and rhythm as early as any instrument did, or any voice, or any foot on a porch board. I know you'll believe me when I say I know about what ceases to be and what goes on without cease. Human animals cease to be. Trees and music go on forever.

A woman named Georgie Smythe gave me a little jack knife on my sixth birthday. She turned over her pail and sat on it, tapped her foot on the dirt. I sat. She showed me how to hold the knife edge against the skinny neck of the stringbean and press it against my thumb just so. *Thup*. Now turn your wrist and pull it down. *Sip*. Georgie's middle knuckles were big and crooked like creek rock. I loved the way she laughed with her mouth shut, always through her nose.

In my home, we'd used our thumb and finger to snap the beans. We'd not used a knife. When the knife's edge touched my thumb, I felt something I can't name. It was a thing I'd foreverafter chase.

Thup Sip Thup Sip Thup Sip

I strung beans faster than Georgie by the time I was eight. Faster than Aunt Jane by nine. I hummed melodies all around the *Thup*

Sip, so constant was its meter. It guided my mornings and sang me to sleep and, sometimes, it was there when I awoke.

The knife's blade had to be kept just so. If it was too dull, you'd overpress and cut your thumb. If it was too sharp, you'd come clean through the head and cut your thumb.

My Aunt Ida never strung a bean in her life and she smoked a pipe morning to night. She said very little and wore sorrow in her eyes and mouth. But Ida was a knife grinder down at the trading spot, and that's how we met Georgie. Ida wore a big field hat to keep the sun off her shoulders and sat on a piece of lumber she set on the ground. Never looked anyone in the eyes and always had a peculiar smell, like rancid butter and old wet mushrooms. Ida could sharpen your blade, and she undercut every man's asking price to do it. The speed and rhythm she maintained on her wheel hypnotized her patrons. I was little enough to sit cross-legged by her pedal foot and look up at the sparks flying. I let them fall on the backs of my hands. My arms. I learned not to flinch.

Ida's hands were marked by tiny glimmering specks of skin. Fire's Kiss, we called it. Her fingernails were outlined in silver and black.

After Georgie gave me the knife, it was Ida who showed me how to really sharpen, both rough and fine. She showed me how to straighten, how to strop.

Ida was the only white woman I knew in those early times who openly stood against slavery. It was one of the few topics on which she would converse. "A thing from hell's belly," she said. "None can be owned." I never heard my mother say such a thing, nor my Aunt Jane. When such talk commenced, their lips tightened and they just kept on braiding their garlic. They stood up and stomped to the porch and hung the bushels in the rafters to dry.

Georgie Smythe was the first Black woman I knew and she was the only person Ida talked to at the trading spot. My mother and Aunt Jane didn't even know Georgie and yet they spoke about her in a foul manner I recognized as wrong the first time I heard it. Ida told me they learned this talk from a bad uncle back home, and from the men at the tobacco market and the cooperage and the blacksmith and the druggist.

Georgie sold eggs and herbs. When no one was around, she told Ida about her life. These were the only times I remember Ida's pipe going cold.

At dinner one night, Ida told mother and Aunt Jane what had happened to Georgie's family, how she was only seven when they were traded to the white men for caskets of brass kettles and brandy, how they were stacked and manacled inside a slave ship, how she awoke in blackness one morning to feel her mother—still chained to her—stiff and cold and knocking about from the waves, how she screamed then and heard her father roar back from a deck below, how her father refused to eat after that so they held his mouth open to force it in, how—before he starved to death—he bit off a white finger and thumb and spat them to the boards, and Georgie landed in the colony alone and marched with strangers in a coffle to the block, where she was sold to a man who raped her for most of her young life after that, until he sold her to a Methodist man, who allowed her to buy her freedom. This was far and away the most talking I'd ever heard from Ida.

Then it was quiet.

Jane set down her fork so hard she bent the copper tines. She said she was going to the creek to check the lines. She took the lantern and the rest of us sat in the dark. Ida started to say something further. My mother told her to shut her mouth.

When I was eleven, Ida left early one June morning for the trading spot and no one ever saw her nor Georgie again.

I cried alone for the first two days. Nobody checked on me. I went to the kitchen on the third day and sat down and started stringing half-runners and listening to Aunt Jane and Mother talk about drought and rain and how best to keep your eyes down around menfolk. I used my knife. They used nothing.

Thup Sip

I hear it still. It's the sound of the blood washing in and out of my chambers and caves. It is old music. I hear it where I lie right now, on my back in this bed I made from storm wood. There is writing on the ceiling above me. Can you read what it says? Are you the one who wrote it?

At night, before she was gone, I'd sometimes find Ida at the big oak table with a split seam cup of chicory coffee in her hands. She'd ask if I had my knife on me. I'd hand it over and she'd thumb the blade. If I'd kept up with the metal, she'd say, "Good."

I've kept up ever since. There are men with inch-thick muscle across their carotids and jugulars. There are men whose blood still carries the enslaver's tune.

I was always an assassin and my only chief was me.

SONG OF THE BAD PRIZE

The old woman named my burden. She who once drank heeyoo-chul, she who had been a cello virtuoso, a theremin master.

I'd begun confiding in her as I am wont to do over the years when I get close to a particular kind of woman. I start to tell on myself a little, particularly if I've been smoking buckwheat. That day, I told of my cursegift as plain as possible. I said: "When I meet someone's eye, even for the very first time, I understand them. If I take their hand, it's stronger. I might know what made them how they are."

She was building a theremin from bamboo and scrapmetal. It would run on solar. None thought it possible, but the old woman did. "That ain't possible, old woman," they said. "Fuck you," she told them.

It was fall of 2023, the early days on Buckwheat Mountain. The old woman's name was Zizi Kozma. I loved her, for more than any other, she reminded me of Auntie Eel. I will tell you about Auntie Eel another time.

Zizi Kozma chewed a root I couldn't name. A doubled blue tarp beneath her knees where she worked. We were out in front of her cabin and it was springtime. There were birds then, and they were calling. Zizi Kozma's bony wrist turned expertly as she bore down on a screw atop her theremin cabinet. When it was tightened, she looked up at me. "What you got is the Bad Prize."

How's that?

And she rid herself of the root, stabbed her Phillips head clear through the tarp to the dirt, stood, and proclaimed a lunch break.

She'd winced as she stood. Her wrists worked fine but her hips knees and ankles were shot. I followed her to the cabin. She put considerable weight on her cane and spoke loudly as she limped along. "The Bad Prize," she said. "Means you're blessed, but your blessing brings you pain."

Inside, she put coffee on the cookstove and sat down in a wicker chair. I sat opposite. She looked me in the eyes. There was just enough light from the window to see. She'd wallpapered the place in horizontal strips. It was old paper, covered in helical columns of redbirds chasing a needle and thread. The coffee steamed. Zizi stirred it with a stick. She was always gifted at conversing beyond long silences. "The pain is theirs but then it's yours too," she said.

Yes.

* * *

"You remember when me and you first met?" she asked.

Yes.

"Mosestown."

Yes, it was.

"At Paulie and Ancie's place on 9th Avenue."

Paulie and Ancie is what everyone called Paul and Ancella Knox, and their brick four square on 9th Avenue and Pease Street was home to so many of the greats in those good ole bad ole days.

"In the backyard," she went on, holding her eyes in that way only saturated drunks can earn. She smiled. "I was in the baby pool with a frozen margarita."

I said: "If memory serves, you were naked."

She laughed. "As a jaybird."

It was the summer before little donnie trump ascended. Zizi had gotten sloppy drunk and I'd wrapped her in a big Garfield towel. I remember how it looked stretched across her shoulders, orange and yellow red, gluttonous Garfield foundering on lasagna again. I held her hands that night in the dark corner of the yard behind the sycamore tree. She cried and cried. She must have said the word *fuckin* a hundred times.

Zizi's son Albert was Stanley's best friend. I watched Albert that night as he danced the old familiar dance of noticing his drunk mother, pretending not to notice his drunk mother. He picked up his own children by their ankles and dipped their beautiful heads of hair into the baby pool water where the grass blades circled. Upside-down laughter is good laughter, particularly when it emanates from the belly of a four-year-old child.

Covid killed Albert in December of 2020 at the age of forty-six. No one could tell Zizi about her son because no one knew where she was.

She had disappeared again after that backyard day in 2016, and she'd only come back to us seven years later, after we moved to the mountain, after the Covid and the big storm the great flood. No one could believe she was still alive.

In her cabin, on that fall day of her final year, we held hands again. She told me she had some homemade hooch tucked away for a special occasion. I said every day alive was such a time. She smiled. And before she went to get that cloudy jar, her eyes were steady for a moment, a voltaic moment with a cello virtuoso, a coaxer of the theremin, a beautiful human animal who never could stiffen her drinking wrist and straighten up and fly right. In her steady eyes was a song. I could see it spinning forth from the iris in measures, and when it was near enough, I took its pain and made it my own. I was glad to do it, for I cherished talking to Zizi Kozma. She was probably eighty in 2023, and what I most cherished was how she thought of me as her contemporary, maybe even a little younger than her. So many times over the years, I've loved talking to old women who think they are older than me. It frees them to speak their truest minds.

I've only ever told twelve people about my inability to die. In the old old days when they called me Evry, I had to go on the run and rename myself and wait for folks to die off, and then I was called

Winny, and I had to run and rename and wait on death all over again. Then I was Sal for a while. Been Betty Baach ever since.

When you're with one family long enough, it comes clear that you have to tell. So over the years I told Chesh and Abe and Goldie and Ben and Eel and Ancella and Paul and Dot and Rimmy and Stan. I told Memphis when she turned sixteen, on the night I gave her the embroidered linen shirt I'd made. To tell such a truth to someone so young was admittedly premature on my part, but I knew she was one of the few who needed to know. You don't want to tell something like that to just anyone, but Memphis Knox was not just anyone. I loved her from the moment of her birth, so little and perfect and named as she was for Memphis Tennessee Garrison, who had been a mentor in McDowell to so many Black girls and boys and men and women—Lissa's mother among them—in those hard old times.

Once, in the hot sodden August of 2019, I told my truth to some-one I shouldn't have and it broke hell loose. A couple other times, I was on the precipice of telling the wrong kind of people, but I was lucky enough to have built in me a thickening mass of gas and, as such, in both cases, I elected instead to fart loudly and thereby change the course of history.

I have already told you: I just keep rumbling.

SONG OF THE FISHBIRD

I was fifty-seven-years old when I first saw two worlds at once. I was sitting outside my home in a chair. This was when I lived up the Cut, on land they later called Bonecutter Ridge. I loved that place, all alone in my clearing in the deep wood. There was so much sweetgum around me there, and at that time of year, a wall of sweetgum trees at sundown was almost like staring at a fire.

It was warm for October. I stretched my legs as I sat, crossed one over the other. I'd spent the day picking up sweetgum balls and hacking from every branch the ones that hadn't dropped. I used a big blackened cutlass sword I'd once taken off a man on the banks of Lake Pontchartrain. The sword had an iron grip.

The sweetgum seeds made a tea that kept you regular and held all sickness at bay.

I stabbed that naval sword in the dirt beside my chair and cursed not a little. I had believed in my gut that Cornstalk would put Lewis down but it had not come to be. Word had reached me that morning. The battle upriver was lost. The takers of the land would keep coming.

I looked at the yard. After I'd cut down the seed pods, I'd slashed the stick weeds and stomped on the shoots. It was big as a ball field and shaped in a circle. I admired its curvature and drank homemade wine.

The chair I sat in was made by a man who lived in the woods at the head of the hollow. He'd built it from vine he'd cut. That vine was as big around as your wrist. I remember I had a book on my lap about the Water Lynx and its copper-scaled tail. Back then reading could still keep me from bad luck and trouble.

I'd no sooner read one sentence when here came that ole chair-maker again, limping quick from the dark of the big trees, sweating in his rag sacks. He carried his chair on a rope over his back.

I regarded him. Kept my legs crossed.

The man couldn't talk. He always grunted and pushed you around and indicated with his hands that you ought to sit in the chair he'd made and then pay him with some tobacco or how about three eggs.

He rolled the chair off his back and stooped over it while he freed the leg. His head was bald and deeply suntanned, his white beard went every which way. He straightened and looked at me. He grunted and pointed and patted his hand on the seat.

I took out my pouch and lit my pipe slow. I stood up and blew smoke at his face and told him I'd sit in it when I was good and ready.

And after I'd walked nine times around my circle, I sat down in the new chair. It was sticky to the touch and smelled like deer shit. His tying vines were too dry.

I looked up at him and started to say it was comfortable, that he could have some eggs and herbs. Beyond him in the woods, a flash of something small and black. The chair gave way with a resounding crack. I dropped, and the rush in my belly swept all the way up my throat and into my face, and just as it reached my eyes, just as my tailbone hit ground, there was an explosion in my field of vision. It blossomed as if by bellows. In the distance, a faint dark horizon line moved like water. I saw right through the mute man—faint sketch of bone, no rags no flesh—and the sweetgums beyond were so red I had to squint my eyes, and everywhere along the tree line, little black fishbirds darted betwixt trunks and branches.

It is difficult to describe these fishbirds. They are only flashes. They are like short sections of black ribbon and they move with beautiful grace, curling uniformly. They tuck away wherever they please, always silent. You will forever wonder if you saw them or not, whilst I—since October 11, 1774—no longer have to wonder. I've been seeing them ever since.

I've seen them in the old woods and in the new. They did not die when the knot bumpers clearcut every hill. I've seen them in Baltimore and in Spain. I've seen them glide the surface of Lake Pontchartrain.

For a time I thought the fishbirds were seraphim. I had good reason. It happened on Christmas night, 1938. I will tell it to you.

Something bad was rising and I'd been feeling dark again so I visited an old woman up the Cut who some folks believed was a healer. She lived inside a shack with a cat-and-clay chimney. She made me a tea of what looked to be waxy mushroom caps and crushed seeds of morning glory. I drank it down. We sat in silence for an hour and when she finally opened her mouth to speak, every sound she made spelled out in white letters on the air, but the letters were shapes I couldn't recognize, building words I'd never know. I'd had magic mushrooms and cactus juice both, but nothing ever so strong as this.

I walked outside and collapsed onto my back under a cold night sky. I turned my head to vomit. Everything pulsated and convulsed. The fishbirds did figure eights around dead frozen milkweed chutes with gray empty pods. I watched the chutes turn green, and the whole field burst alive as if it were June. White tufts leaped from glistening coronas and carried forth to the dark sky where hunting fishbirds descended in tight-aligned columns and snatched the tufts in flight, and crunched upon their spiny masts, and banked hard right and rolled and rolled and rolled away.

I closed my eyes. When I opened them again, I saw as if through a slow-motion stereotelescope—two big panels of magnified-microscopic air above me—and inside the panels, I could see with

startling clarity that each darting fishbird was an eight-winged
smoky angel. Worry and fear came upon me then.

The fishbirds finished their feasting and rested on the branches
of the trees.

I closed my eyes. When I opened them again, the ground beneath
me was black lumber. Painters' tape x-marks to my right and left.
I was on my belly and I slid a little, gripped the wood with my
fingers and toes. It was a raked stage, and standing at the high end
was a clown-faced costumed man, painted gills on his suit jacket,
eight wire wings strapped to his back.

It was very quiet save for a single cough. It had not come from the
costumed man. There was an audience out in the dark.

He walked to me. His feet were bare. He sat on his heels and
cupped his mouth with his hand and whispered in my ear: "One
hundred years from this very night. That is when it ends." He
smelled of beeswax and lanolin. I looked up at his caked white
makeup, cracking at his stubbled chin. His lips were done in a
blood red frown. His painted black mustache curled on the ends.
He smiled. He said, "Que cliché, no?"

From his nosehole a nightcrawler came forth, and it waggled and
searched the stale air. From his mouth when he spoke, a single
fishbird emerged, and then it was no longer there.

I closed my eyes. When I opened them again, I was in the cabin
of the old woman, seated and wrapped in buckskin blankets beside
the cat-and-clay oven. I could smell the ginseng tea she brewed.

Of all the times I've seen the fishbirds, Christmas 1938 has most
barbed the dart. Its clearcut century's claim on time has left me

eyeing a singular date: the night of December 25, 2038. Christmas of this very year.

After trump and Covid and the big storm and the flood, after the sheer speed and terror of the time when we came to live on the mountain, I thought of that date more and more. One night, drunk on shine, I told Rimmy and Dot of the costumed painted man in my vision and what he'd said. We laughed and laughed. Dot said that if we made it to December 26, 2038, we'd toast the dawn with the hid-away lightning—that ole Mingo shine, that ole one-batch hooch what could send you flying—and we'd sing the old song, and dance the old dance.

I don't really think we'll wake up dead on December 26. I think mushrooms grown in dwarf-goat shit are not to be trusted with the fate of the world. Wildflowers choked on coke-oven ash will inevitably birth bad seeds. I was fooled by the old woman's tea. The fishbirds are not time nor death. I know the truth now: just like every other time I've seen them, the fishbirds were silent that Christmas in 1938. It was not their voice I heard from the man, though a fishbird surely flew from his mouth as he spoke.

They have never made a sound. They only swim and hide, watch and listen and feed. They bear witness to the terrible voice of relinquished time. They give respite and carry war's sounds away on the water, which is the blood of the earth, circulating, remembering itself. Everything comes back in time, just as the Arrow will. Just as the mantis and the tree. The water in Sharp Creek travels to the sea. It carries its memories across the world, only to switch back and return again to Sharp Creek.

Cornstalk surrendered and I fell through the mute man's chair. My vision exploded much like it did when I was choked at the hands of Sol Wood. Here is what I know: ever since Sol Wood choked me I have had the same ninety-nine dreams, and ever since I fell through the mute man's chair, I have seen two worlds at once. I glance at a quarter-pane of doorglass and see a jut-toothed man. I walk past a rhododendron and there's a raccoon in its shadow, washing the seed of a plum. I stare at an old coat of paint at the dentist's, and plain as day, hanging flat from four tacks, are four skunk pelts.

I remember clearly the day of the skunk pelts. One of the grandbabies was back in the hydraulic chair for sealants when *snap-crackle-pop!* here came the pelts upon the khaki dentist drywall. The office was being redecorated. Nothing but nail holes and sun streaks. It must have been 2020, for I remember I was wearing the rainbow-fist facemask my niece made for me. I could smell those skunk pelts through my mask though it was triple-layered. I laughed out loud at the sight and smell of them, same as I laughed in church pews at the guest cards.

A woman across the waiting room looked up from her *Entertainment Weekly* and eyeballed me. And then would you believe this white woman without a mask tried to stare me down for having laughed, or for having laughed whilst wearing a mask during a pandemic, or for having laughed whilst wearing a mask during a pandemic that signaled love and empowerment of Black and brown and gay and trans people? It didn't occur to her that she might just smile and look back to her magazine, or maybe even ask me what was funny so that I might spread my joy her way. She kept right on with the skunk eye instead. What a world we lived in. This woman was throwing skunk eye, and yet she could not see the skunks. I should have told her, "Honey, don't miss the skunks for the paint," but I didn't have the energy to set her straight. I just told her the plain truth instead. I said: "You see that dread khaki wall right there?" And I pointed at the wall, and she wisely abandoned her unwise attempt at being hard, and turned her head, and looked upon it.

I see four skunks tacked on that wall.

SONG OF RECURRING DREAM #44

Me and a tall man run on wrenched ankles, headlong into the cow pasture where a single llama stands in the washed-out northeast corner, digging a trench to escape. Above him, on a shagbark limb, a painter skulks low-necked. I try to scream warning but no sound will issue. I turn to the man where he runs next to me. His lips are sewn shut but I can read his mind. It's always three words on repeat: *Wide vision ambush!* When I turn back to the corner of the pasture, it's too late. The llama is not there. In his place, a row of half-runners grows. I see only the big cat's haunches as she arcs over the fence, dark form hung from her unseen mouth, paintstroke streaking across unseen night.

I aim at the ear of sweet Rimmy Knox and sing in a falsetto all the songs of my dreams.

SONG OF BLOOD

How the wind did whistle in the wood as they walked John Brown to the gallows. How the fingers of the hangman trembled.

The hood must be secured in place before the noose is looped, but the wind that day snagged the hood, and the hangman could not fit his implement.

Old John Brown pulled from his lapel three straight pins and gave them to the hangman, and the hangman fit the hood with the pins and looped the noose and pulled his handle, and sprung the door.

Oh, how the detonation of a thousand radiant moons fills the skull, throat, breast, and belly. Bolts of fire issue the limbs. See how the arms pulse and pulse once more before the stillness takes.

A body that carried such lightning could never lie a-mouldering for long.

I was on a ridge that day, my Kentucky rifle tucked into my shoulder, my cheek laid on the stock. I breathed deep but I did not squeeze the trigger. I just stared, one-eyed, at that hangman and his straight clean platform built for death. I knew that if I killed the hangman, another would only take his place straightaway and pull the handle, and if they couldn't get to me quick enough, I might shoot that one too, but still another man was at the ready, and he'd leap to the platform too, and he would drop John Brown without a second thought.

I could never forget the sound of that sprung trap door.

Back when there were restaurants and junior high jazz band concerts, before tablets and mobile phones, parents would occupy the little ones with endless games of hangman. It was a remarkable teacher of spelling and penmanship. "Don't press so hard, Sugar. You'll tear the napkin."

I used to save them, the napkins and the scraps of paper placemats. Only one remains, and it is my favorite. I keep it in breastpocket #9. It is the work of the small, precise hand of Memphis Knox. Black ink on the back of a menu from Mei's Chinese Buffet on 8th Street. I believe she was five at the time. I can still see her smile as I solved the word and the stick man escaped his sentence of death.

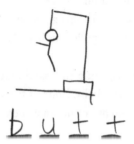

Memphis always chose an easy word. She had to be sure that no stick man was ever fully formed, no final leg or length of foot drawn. She'd add two eyes, a nose, and a mouth if need be. She'd give him a curly mustache just to be sure he didn't dangle.

After she was gone, after we'd finally found her, the coroner could not pinpoint what time Memphis was struck on the short gravel shoulder of Dug Hill Road. Nor could he name the hour of her death in relation to being struck. Only a date was given. August 21.

She was found on the 24th.

*   *   *

She'd ended up twenty yards from the roadway, down a high-weed embankment, where a mountain biker saw the bottom of her foot as he crested his Tuesday trail route.

The boy at the wheel had never stopped. He came forward on Thursday after the TV news went from search-party story to mourning story to investigative story. The boy's name was Pinch Turnbuck. He was twenty. He said he had no recollection of hitting anything with his black Nissan Armada, its right headlamp staved, its custom front grille cracked to pieces. He was just another one who couldn't remember what he'd done because he couldn't wait until he got home to fix up. Like so many before him, he'd fixed in his vehicle, out front of his dealer's, and then he'd thrown the shifter into drive and set out for home.

Memphis had graduated high school the same year as Pinch. She'd known him. We all knew the Turnbucks—even back then, before all the coming trouble—and my own history twines with theirs back to 1855, all of it a dark affair. I don't have the breath to cover such territory, but it will come to light. I imagine nearly everything will come to light in time.

In April of 2012, we built a community garden in Memphis's name, right there in the empty gravel lot next to Shoeless Joe's Skillet Chicken, the best eating spot in Mosestown. Stan's old friend Rigo Rivas had just bought the restaurant from the Preece sisters and was happy to host and cater the garden's grand opening, complete with large-scale mural unveiling and live music. Children from the neighborhood built those beds and kept those vegetables. There were six big whiskey barrels in a line, three-quarters full of dirt. There were three long-trough planters, and yardstick stakes linked by slacked twine, suspension bridges built for stinkbugs.

The children laminated identification tags and stuck them in the dirt. I loved their penmanship. *Asparagus. Rhubarb. Sorrel.*

The lacquered wooden sign at the crest was subtle and plain and made by the magnificent hands of Barbara Ailes.

A Community Garden
In Loving Memory
of Memphis Tennessee Knox.

Barbara had also painted the restaurant's original picture-window sign.

Shoeless Joe's Skillet Chicken
If you fry it, they will eat

We used to go to Shoeless Joe's every Friday and Sunday, and Rigo would feed us off-the-menu-on-the-house, spice so hot you cried like a baby. We'd laugh and laugh out there in Memphis's garden. At the back was a brick wall. On the brick wall was a mural. Barbara and Rimmy painted it together, ten feet by twelve. It is the kind of paint on brick that holds your eye and calls to mind the old cave paintings. In it, Memphis flies with the birds in her white linen shirt, her hair in horizontal tornadoes, trailing behind. She soars across a bright blue sky, hand in hand with her namesake.

I am trying to save every life I can.

SONG OF THE ARROW

It was the day the birds came back to us. That's what we ended up calling that day. The Arrow.

July the 8th, 2033. They came at dusk. I was smoking buckwheat on the hill by the spring house, leaning on a lion's head cane. Four or five children had trailed me from the fire. I pointed uphill to a big gray outcrop and said, "Children! Keep your eyes peeled for Side-Hill-Gougers!"

I was all the time reading to the children from *Kickle Snifters and Other Fearsome Creatures* back then, riffing my own way on Bill Dads and Windigo and Squidgicum Squee, designating a day each child could be Mule McSneed. I pointed at storm-shattered trees on our hikes and called out their name: "Splintercats!" I explained to the children that there was never any Gowrow behind the curtain, that there was only an old woman roaring and screaming and banging on a pan and firing a gun in the air.

The day the Arrow came, I was telling them a story I'd made up on the spot about cannibals who ate their meals on fine china. I believe I was describing the bent tines of a copper fork when I first heard the sound. It came faint, like an old steam whistle when the westward wind was right. The children heard it too. They squinted and shaded their eyes with their little hands and looked up and waited, and none of us gave one thin damn about those cannibals anymore, because we were living the story of our lives, and here came the Arrow, and this was something you felt in the pith of your bones.

The whistle grew to a whoosh, and when the formation came free of the high tree canopy and filled our vision, we dropped our cupped hands and opened our eyes wide. The birds had blocked out the sun.

Though their cast shadow was dark, these were not blackbirds. Nor were they vultures or hawks. These were warblers and whip-poor-wills and titmice. Wood thrushes, nuthatches, all the littlest birds we thought were gone, all the souls who'd long since flown to their fiery deaths, called to the radial core of the sun's love. Now here they were, back again by the thousands. Their flocks interlocked, their songs grafted and called all at once. Their shape an arrow as big as four football fields.

Of the 117,321 days I've lived, the Arrow is my most favorite.

We were all of us still and silent as we watched it undulate, moving east over Hogback Ridge. There it slackened and put on the drag, and then it turned like the slow-motion tail of a bullwhip's crack, and aimed itself straight for us. Here came the Arrow, descending, descending, and then, at Eastern Tower's perimeter, breaking open at beaked point and rolling apart in helical sections, each bird alighting on a sighted tall tree.

Nine thousand such trees Freon Hill now boasts, and so it was that no bird needed to land on the ground, nor even a low bough. They sank the treetops. They lined the high limbs, a hundred on each branch, fifty to a sprig.

The trees groaned and cracked and popped. A shiver emanated outward from every trunk, rolling forth through the ground and underneath our feet. It tickled. The children—heretofore silent and still—jumped and giggled.

Then the birds went quiet all at once. The mesmerizing bounce of the high limbs slowed. For a moment, it was as if the birds were the missing thing the trees had long sought. Two pieces of the same being, reunited, and the children knew not to jump or giggle, but just to keep watching and listening.

It may have stayed this way for three to five seconds. It seemed longer, of course. A thing like that doesn't just skip on by.

Then the first of the calls came, high and shrill. Then another. And another. They built exponentially like this until we had to cover our ears with our hands. No theremin or drum could ever mimic this tune. It was a war song.

The thrushes and whip-poor-wills dove, and then the warblers and titmice flitted. They snatched every snail and spider from every spruce in sight. They yanked every worm and grub from every tilled row, every composted mound. Praying mantises raised their arms to fight and were torn to pieces by the zipping butcher birds. Mosquitoes and moths and butterflies ceased to be on the air, which had itself become a swirling, singing thing. A living gyre before our very eyes. And sections of the gyre began to move in ways that shaped littler things. Bison, rocking chairs, faces of unknown origin.

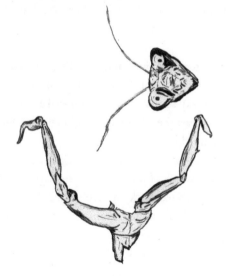

And I saw in one such formation the trembling lip of a child, and my throat seized.

The Arrow was difficult for the human eye to behold. I saw one little boy lean against the spring house and throw up. Several children sat down or simply toppled. More reported later on feeling sick and dizzy, though they kept their stance and held down their lunch.

For me it was all of my visions come at once, fishbirds and whirling flashes of tree and light, but this time it was immeasurably magnified. It was magnificent. And this time, I was not alone. Everyone around me saw what I saw.

Their feasting lasted no more than a minute or two, and then they ascended to the high limbs again, and sang their belching quiet tunes as the limbs bobbed beneath, and down below we human animals mumbled and exclaimed and hugged and walked all around the place looking for evidence of any bug left alive. We didn't find a one.

The sun went down and the birds remained, quiet and full. We lay on our backs in the field and watched them. We drank homemade wine and kept our fire small.

Just before midnight the intermittent calls grew sharp and loud. The treetops lifted as the birds took flight again, this time against the black night sky so that we could not make out their formation, and to the east they drove, beyond Hogback Ridge, beyond whatever remained.

There was endless talk of the Arrow in the days, weeks, months, and years to come. Small flocks of warblers and thrushes did return right away, but only a few stayed on.

* * *

The keepers of the crops complained about all of the stolen worms, about the depletion of their soil's richness at the beaks and claws of the birds. I thought they ought to keep their mouths shut about it and remain in awe of what we'd witnessed, but human animals will inevitably complain.

In fall and winter, some of the children put out seed and suet. By night, it generally got eaten and, in the day, there was a noticeable uptick in high-canopy birdsong but, still, there was nothing like the Arrow.

The children asked me every day: "BigMom, do you think the Arrow will come again?

I always answered the same: "I believe it will."

Children, I believe it will come again.

SONG OF THE RUNAWAYS

They came on the Ohio in the morning dark. Low fog moved crosscurrent on the water. They got within fifty yards, six of them facedown on the scrapwood ferry. Come on a little faster now, I prayed to the unknown gods. There had been little rain in over a week and the current was slow.

Way upriver on opposite bank, a hot lantern swung, then went still. There was the far-off sound of a man's quick shout, and then of a flatboat hitting the water, and then nothing. The lantern had been put out. I listened for boat oars straining. I had the bad feeling again.

One of the ferry's six sat up on her knees when they got inside twenty yards. She carried a pack on her back. The shepherd threw her the post rope, and she caught it and tied it to the ferry's long knot, and the shepherd reeled them in.

I bellied down on the dry grass and tucked the butt of my Kentucky rifle to my shoulder. I kept my eyes on the water, save to glance at the rope catcher when she reached me, first one up the path, quiet as a mouse. She was a tall woman. What I'd seen on her back was a sleeping baby slung tight.

I whispered: "How many tracking you?"

"Two," she whispered back.

The shepherd led the rest of them up the path quick and quiet. They all looked straight ahead.

* * *

I asked her if she knew the catchers.

"Torts brothers," she said. "They very very bad."

I knew the name well, and I'd heard what unspeakable thing they'd done to a child at Greenbottom. I said, "I didn't hear any dog. Do they have a dog?"

"No dog," the rope catcher said.

It was 1860 and the people had told the story of John Brown's attempt over and again. Black people told it one way and white people another, and I have watched that tradition continue right on up to now.

I saw more passengers that year than any before it. When I'd first started on the railroad, I was a conductor. I'd meet them at the waystation and ferry them across to Burlington, but I soon made clear to the stationmaster what job better suited me, and he put me on the Ohio side, bellied down if need be. He was different from most on the underground. He knew old ways.

I thanked the tall quiet woman with the baby on her back and she followed the others up the path. She had eyes that reminded me of Georgie Smythe's and my heart beat *thup sip*. I peaked at the cloud cover above. The moon would come free shortly. I put my cheekbone to the stock, and when they emerged at two hundred yards—two dark stumps in the fog—I shut my left eye and sighted with my right, and exhaled, and squeezed. My eye foresaw the bore's helical path and followed it home. One stump stood. My reload was ten seconds. Exhale, squeeze. No stumps stood.

Most nights the boat was empty when I snagged it on down the riverbank, as I only ever fired strafing shots, plunking the water within inches of their vessel so they might jump ship and swim back to whence they came. But this night was different. I'd heard what those brothers had done at Greenbottom.

Their craft came in snagging distance and I hooked it with a fallen limb.

Neither catcher had slipped limp into the black water because each had died as he dropped. I picked them clean: two rifles, two pistols, two half-full flasks, and four tins of fish. I lashed them tight with fifty-pound shore rocks, and took us out to the middle again, and rolled them in.

The moon was fully free of the clouds by then and the sun would be up in an hour. I said a prayer of thanks to the unknown gods that there had been no dog. Other nights, I'd not been so lucky, but in all those runaway years, I never once had to harm a catcher's dog. Had to muzzle a few until they'd settled down, but they were mostly just tired from having swum to shore, or sometimes scared, having ridden to me on a boat with no owner. They all came around in the end. Dogs aren't men. Dogs will change if you love them hard enough.

I don't know how many Ohio River crossings I worked, but I'll never forget what made me seek them in the first place, for it happened at the river, too, and I'll tell it to any West Virginian who pretends this state is somehow different, who says white people here were somehow gentler than the those to our south.

It was 1855. There had been a drought and then a deluge. Bad season for tobacco. Farming families who were in debt and looking to free up cash took to selling property. I got word at dawn from a tinker that a family named Turnbuck was fixing to sell two children right from under their mother, a woman whose husband they'd sold two years prior, a woman who'd been with the Turnbucks for fifteen years and raised their six white children on top of raising her own. In order that this white family might outrun bank foreclosure, they would sell her two boys, aged eight and ten, for $1,000 apiece.

It was a sunny cold morning when I came on horseback down Sap Streeet in Guyandotte. A woman was selling soup in an alley. A knife grinder next to her was setting up his wheel. I thought of Ida, her fire-kissed hands. The filthy blacksmith stepped from his shop and lit his pipe. I knew him a little. I nodded hello and asked him about the disgraceful tobacco farmers in question. He told me it was already happening at the docks.

I rode hard but it was too late when I reached the river. From the head of the long landing stairs, I saw the steamboat pulling away, saw the dock man at the cleat tossing the rope. The children were chained on the boat's top deck. I thought about pulling my Kentucky rifle from the saddle scabbard, but there was nothing to be done.

On the dock below, people milled about while the mother of those little boys dropped to her knees and fell on her side. She'd fainted away, and the white men standing all around left her where she lay, and they skipped rocks on the water's surface, and spat.

From out on the belching steamboat's deck, the children shrieked and called to their mother. They were chained to men they'd never seen before, all of them headed to the deep south.

I would never forget the sound of those children shrieking.

SONG OF THE MARVELOUS MUSEUM

If I hum these tunes with my mouth shut, will you still be able to read the words? I believe in you. I believe if you listen close, you can still make out these words behind my teeth.

I once knew a man what sewed his mouth shut with saltwater-rated fishing line. Did he leave a small opening unsewn for to ingest his tea, his coffee, and his Chesterfield Longs? Yes, he did.

In Baltimore, I knew another man who painted all the screens in his doors and windows, beautiful scenes of hillsides and rainbows. He once painted Jesus on the shore of a lake, giving the finger to the fishermen casting their nets.

The screen painter's body ceased to be at the waist. He was born half a man. He was always more man than most.

Who decides if a human animal merits a ballad or an anthem or a dirge? How much skin does a woman have to put in the story to keep from being written out?

When will the children know "The Ballad of Magnolia" or "The Anthem of Ida the Moleta" or "The ChantSong of Georgie Smythe" or "The March of Memphis Knox" or "The WarSong of Auntie Eel" or "The LoveSong of Ancella Knox"?

I will never have time to tell of them all.

But I've promised you one or two. Right now I bet you need a LoveSong, so a LoveSong you will have.

Ancella Knox had a maiden name and that maiden name was Baach.

Ancella ended up in Mosestown but she came from McDowell. I knew her daddy Ben Baach a little, her Aunt Agnes. I knew her Great-Uncle Abe, and I knew ole Goldie too. When I relocated to Keystone in 1912, the money still flowed. I stepped off the train on a cold March morning and walked up Wyoming Street with a brand-new name and a suitcase in each fist. A handsome young man waited by a blue-painted door, and in his hand was a big skeleton key to open the saloon I'd been hired to run. "Morning, ma'am," he said. "I'm Chesh."

"Pleased to meet you, Chesh. I'm Betty Baach."

It was the first time I'd said the new name aloud. Before that, everybody called me Sal.

*   *   *

Funny thing about the Baaches, you could be one whether you were born to them or not. That is how it ought to be with names and families.

Ancella's daddy Ben Baach was born to a young woman who'd become pregnant working Cinder Bottom. She'd split town soon after he was born, and so the Baaches raised him as their own. Some folks talked on it because Ben's mother was Black, and his father presumably white, and so he didn't look much like the rest of the pale Baaches in pictures. Mostly folks just talked on how handsome he was. Ben Baach had eyes green as bottle glass. He wed very young to a Black woman from Keystone and they had one child, Eloise Brandywine Baach (Eel). Then he wed very old to a white woman from Switchback and had four more. Some of the children went on to marry white, some Black, and so it was that the Baaches came in every shade. Auntie Eel always said, "I'm the Blackest Baach alive."

Ancella had the same green eyes as her daddy and she could always see something in somebody, and she always had that big Yashica on a homemade yellow strap around her neck. She'd talk to a man for an hour at the tent village on the creek, and sometimes she'd ask "Would you mind too terribly if I made your picture?," lifting her camera in her hands like an offering, lens cap on.

She won a World Press Photo Award in 1972 for a photograph of a man carrying his elderly mother over a mud bank as they walked the ruined tracks at Buffalo Creek, two houses and a pickup truck stacked mud-black behind them at peculiar angles, the old woman's rain cap caught in the February wind.

Dot, the oldest of Ancella's three children, is named for Dorothea Lange.

Ancella once made a photograph of Bill Withers singing "Use Me" into a birdcage microphone. The photograph hung in the Knox's

9th Avenue kitchen next to a steel rack of scrap-paper cookbooks. It was a beautiful black-and-white photograph. She'd framed it in leftover crown molding spraypainted gold. You could watch people come in the open front door—partying at that old house for the first time—and the Withers portrait would catch their eye, and they'd get closer and closer and they'd say, "Hey, who is this cat? I know this cat."

Ancella would sashay and her cup would runneth over and mark the shag carpet again, and she'd say, "That was 1974 in Los Angeles. I was pregnant with Stanley, working shoots for Michael Ochs." She'd point to a spot of light in the portrait's top-left corner. "See that? That's buckshot."

She'd taken the picture inside a quonset hut near Culver City. During the previous night's jam session, somebody had stood outside and unloaded a shotgun point-blank. "Right next door was an oil rig with a circle of palm trees around it," Ancella would say. She'd put her wine down and set her hands on her hips and commence to vigorously bend at the waist and swing back up, again and again. "Pumpjack!" she'd exclaim. Ancella was always and everywhere doing the Pumpjack and the Shorty George and Spank the Baby too.

In the photograph, Withers's afro is pristine and his mutton chops precise. His eyes are shut tight. Ancella's focus was sharpest upon his left hand, thumb hooked around the rolled guitar neck. He looks like a man born to sing. "I cried after I took it," she would say. "Put my camera away and just cried." He'd sung "I Can't Write Left-Handed" right there in the quonset hut. Her voice quivered when she recalled it: "He called a sound would make anybody cry."

I met Bill Withers only once, a couple of years before he died, and he remembered Ancella, remembered the buckshot tin of the Culver City recording hut. He had eyes that saw and he could set a spell. We talked about Raleigh County, and Mingo and McDowell. We talked about pimiento cheese and half-runners and sweet pickles and the legendary thieving of Doris Payne. He said, "You can't sleep on Slab Fork," and wasn't that the truth.

I would generally advise that you cannot sleep on people from anywhere inside these hills. Remember that about us.

When Bill Withers died, the children were already in the streets of Georgia and Kentucky calling Ahmaud Arbery's name and Breonna Taylor's name, as they'd called so many before, as they would come to call George Floyd's name in two months' time. Soon enough, the children swelled and made rivers out of city thoroughfares and it seemed for a moment that the captains would have no harbor. The children were strong and respectful and Black and white together. And when we old farts starting calling "Lean On Me," swaying on braced knees before the shields of the riot police, the children dutifully raised their lighted smart phones and sang along.

The Withers portrait was one of eighty or more black-and-whites that hung in the 9th Avenue home of the Knoxes of Mosestown. Ancella made them all. About half of that number made it here, and there they are, tacked on yon painted wall.

I can't recall hanging them, but there they are. Note their shapely configuration, their painted scrapyard frames and gargantuan black mats.

A few she blew up big as a bay window; most are eight by ten, a half-dozen the size of a playing card. Some are famous people and some are just the Knoxes. The famous people look regular. The Knoxes of Mosestown look famous.

* * *

Look here. Paul wears a handlebar mustache and holds a twenty-pound catfish, cigarette pinched in his smile.

Dot swings on a big knotted rope in her underwear.

Rimmy stands white-sleeved in a varsity jacket, hands in the pockets of his blue jeans, under a theater marquee advertising XXX.

Stanley sits on a hand-me-down bicycle, skinny, no more than ten. The basketball under one arm is as bald as a scrapyard tire. His ballcap is backwards. His shinbones are mapped in bruises.

All of these beautiful people stared down Ancella's big Yashica as if it wasn't there, as if they could see the rest of her in full bloom behind it, not just the scalp-line part in her hair or the crow's feet of her shut left eye. "Ole Camerahead Baach," Paul used to call her.

In Ancella's work, the Knoxes are who they were. They are freer than any of us can remember.

I will show you every photograph I have.

SONG OF WATER

People do not know what we have up here on the mountain. They think they know, but they don't.

People believe we harvest a thousand pounds of cannabis, on average, per growing season. They believe we water religiously by way of a sophisticated raincatcher system that irrigates on a weighted timer, that we hover and prune, cut and bundle and tie and dry and cure and voila! Come on down to the Buckwheat Mountain Trading Spot, or fhe Trading Spot at Freon Hill! It goes by both names, but whatever you call it we offer such legendary sativa strains as Baguetti Belly and Kicklesnifter Jamboree. Folks come from far and wide and hither and yon, and they ferry with them mower blades and old tractor attachments and Technics turntables converted to solar. All such implements are welcome at the trading spot.

I'll be clear. We do all that hovering and harvesting and such. And we make fair trades at the post and people walk away happy and stay that way. But that ain't all we do.

Unhappy people don't bother with us. This is likely on account of the eight towers on the property's octagonal perimeter, two Buckwheaters to a tower, both of them strapped in long guns with banana clips.

People off the hill say we've stockpiled the good old rounds. They say we smelted all those tossed-away freon jugs into armor and ammo, that said ammo is tucked tight inside those banana clips and said armor is strapped to the Buckwheaters in the towers, their sharp-peaked shoulders and convex chest plates shimmering in the sun. They say that the hollow and the ridge are strategically lined in landmines.

None of this is true. The Buckwheaters in the towers wear scrap-metal and painted rope. They don't have a single round between them. Those banana clips are empty as a soup can in Rat Town.

You let the legend bloom. Everything grows tentacles if you let it be a while.

The truth is that, like everybody else's, our supply of lead is limited. In total, we've got four working firearms housing two to three rounds apiece, all locked inside the red shed by the barn-door basketball goal. Only Rimmy and Dot carry the keys to the red shed. They keep them under cover of shirt, on a chain around their neck, right alongside their emergency whistles, which we all carry in the event that the white nationalists try to ambush us again, or the Turnbucks get brave, or both at once.

We are set up better than most to protect our land. It goes back a long ways, and it deserves protecting. There is a burial mound up beyond the last stand of pines along southwestern edge, likely

Seneca. There is the charred foundation of a building called Hood House, originally intended to be a Methodist retreat, white people only. Look around. It's safe to say ole Preacher Hood went zero for two in the end.

Do you know why it's called Freon Hill? Because from the 1940s all the way up until 1987, people would drive clear up to the head of the access road, pop their trunks, and toss their empty oil cans and refrigerant cannisters and freon jugs and propane tanks over the edge. Low men at the service stations were tasked with the job and began to meet on Friday nights at the top, where they'd drink and smoke and play cards by light of their vehicular headlamps. They coined the mountain's name in this way.

After we'd been here a while, people started calling it Buckwheat Mountain because buckwheat is what we called our weed back when there were phones and everything was codes, and so we just naturally kept calling it that in perpetuity. Word spreads. Names root. A pancake was an ounce. Silver dollar was a quarter, short stack a half. KJ was our top seller, BB number two. That's Kicklesnifter Jamboree and Baguetti Belly.

I remember all those little wearisome words on the screen of my little wearisome burner phone. *Can I get short stack KJ pancake? Is possible to get one silver dollar BB pancake?* We had short stack and tall stack, silver dollar specials, freebie Fridays, emergency Monday flapjack rations for those in need, and, for the VIPs, the pancake supper special.

Folks think they know. We have the buckwheat, and it is good for what ails you. But like I tell the children when they ask me if the internet will ever come back, "Don't miss the forest for the trees," and that is what these folks have done. They have missed the water for the weed.

* * *

What we got up here is a real mineral spring.

Oh, how it flows. I drank directly from it once when no one was around to see. An old woman had told me that if I drank it in this way—or if I filled a desert canteen full and drank it down fast—my bones would hollow out and I'd be able to fly, free as a falcon. So one day I lay back and opened my mouth and let the water rush in, straight from the flat rock source, swallow after swallow after swallow, and four or five minutes later I turned into a llama with two short legs on my right side and two long legs on my left, and I spent a week traversing this mountain, gouging the hillside, going round and round and round. And you and I both know by now that we'll never get to the bottom of anything.

I am a side-hill gouger just like you.

SONG OF THE PANTHER

Once upon a time there was a panther. And I hope you don't mind that I named her Pearly, for that is what I named her. It was October when first I saw Pearly. Black of night and cold in the year of three bloody sevens. I was on the run again for carrying out my duty. Awake at my low fire in the deep wood, listening for them who would come to take my life. I did not hear Pearly. The only way I knew she was there was the moon. When it came free of the clouds, its light reflected in her eyes where she stood, thirty feet off between two spruce trees. I could see the curve of her head, straight light of whisker, a tooth when she yawned.

In a bed of leaves, I lay on my back with my head turned her way. I did not move.

Between us was a skinny slash of pearly everlasting, dead and gray. After a spell, Pearly turned and sauntered away.

In the morning, I fed the fire until it was hip-high. I filled my little brass kettle with the water I'd caught and set it on the hot rock to boil. I walked to the pearly everlasting and took out my knife and cut it at the stalk, three inches up. I ground its parts with a bowl and a spoon. From its stalks and stems, I made tea. From its leaves and flowers, I rolled a smoke.

There I sat, drinking my tea and smoking my flower. I sat for nine hours. I got up and stretched and sat another nine.

I slept and awoke and slept and awoke. Each time, Pearly came and sat in the moonlight between the same two trees. She yawned and licked her forepaw and rubbed it against her face. She turned and sauntered away.

On the third night, I was roused from sleep by the feeling of alternating warmth and cold at my nose. I opened my eyes. Pearly stood over me, her mouth above mine, her nose breathing the air of my own. I did not move. I did not look her in the eyes.

Little light from the embers, little light from the moon. I watched the muscles in her shoulder roll when she shifted her weight. I watched the fine beautiful wave of her yellowbrown coat.

She opened her mouth as if to yawn again. When it was wide, she bent and closed her jaw around my throat.

Her canines gripped the skin of my neck, four perfect points pressed at the edge of everything.

I could not breathe. I looked at her eye. It was fixed on the little red embers ahead. I could see their light dance in her black pupil slash. Her ear moved in tune with the sound of the treetop wind, the beetles cutting dirt.

*   *   *

She held me like this until she didn't, and she released and lifted her paw to her tongue, and rubbed her eye, and set the heavy paw back down upon my belly. Then she turned from me and began to dig, moving around me in a circle, kicking up the fallen leaves onto my body, working a perimeter until I was covered. And then she turned, and sauntered away.

I stayed as I was, buried alive. There was a hole in the leaf cover just above my left eye. I could see the high skinny limbs, dead black blood vessels waving to the empty clouds. A peeper called out though it was not spring.

After considerable time, I lifted my arms through the leaves and felt at my throat for the four points. I found them, and I kept my fingertips there for further considerable time.

I stood and the leaves fell around me in an oval. I used them to get the fire going again. I sat and fed the fire and got warm. I could not do anything but laugh until the sun came up. They were coming for me. It was time to leave that place.

Ever since, I've searched in every forest stretch I traversed. I combed that same swath at Backbone Ridge. I slept overnight in the very spot, thrice. I never saw Pearly again. But a panther unseen is still there.

I hear Pearly breathing every time I hold my breath.

SONG OF BONE

Do you know why I miss ice cubes the way I do? I'll tell you why. In the summertime, I've always suffered a good bit of swelling in my knuckles and my knees. I used to put ice cubes in a wet wrung washcloth and tie it around my knuckles. I'd do the same with dishtowels and knot two more around my knees, sometimes my ankles too. The water at the spring is good and cold, but it won't take down your swelling like a cube. When August hangs on and the humidity sticks in the bald, more than just about anything I can call to mind, I miss ice cubes.

I miss grocery stores and takeout lo mein and the way you could drive around in your vehicle listening to Frank Stowers's wondrous voice on West Virginia Public Radio, guessing to yourself how old he was, what he looked like, whether or not he'd fought in a war. Were I able to have that back, I would not portend to be picky. It could be classical hour on a patchy FM signal, it could be "angel is the centerfold" on the AM dial, I don't care. Just put me behind the wheel of a '58 Eldorado and turn me loose.

In the end, I talk sense to myself. A car ain't nothing but a car. An ice cube is just a drop of water froze up. Knuckles and Knees.

Bicycle&Baton. Let's fortify up, every last one. Power to the people. They haven't killed us yet. We walk above ground, not below.

In the hot sodden August of 2029, when you could hardly step outside, my knuckles swole up big as shooter marbles. They pressed against the skin like they'd pop. I'd taken to hiking, seeking high elevation. I had a spot at the mineral spring mouth where I'd lay on my back and hold my hands up high in the wind. I'd dip them in the spring then raise them up. It wasn't ice cubes, but it worked. I was doing this alone on a Friday evening when a woman named ChrissyJo came up the footpath. Part of me knew she was coming to kill me.

"How do, Betty," she said, and sat down near to me.

I'd never cared for ChrissyJo. She'd come to us at the post that spring on a rainy SwapMeet Saturday. She had white-girl dreadlocks and spoke her words in that manner I've never cared for, where the sentences all carry upward as they go. First night on the hill she got drunk and started crying and carrying on. I said even then that something wasn't right. But one of my nieces was sweet on her, so she was allowed overnight, and then Dot ran a check on her and came up empty so we let her stay. But I'd never trusted ChrissyJo.

That evening by the spring she inquired as to my ritualistic hand dipping and raising and I explained about my knuckles.

"You poor thing," she said. Asked if I wanted her to massage my hands.

"Thank you kindly, but no."

She lay down next to me on her back. There was swell of tucked dagger at the base of her spine. "Well, I will pray for you, Betty. I will pray hard as I can for your hands that have done so much for all of us in the movement."

I sure did hate it when people said shit like that. I felt her start to ask a particular question, and I thought: Please don't. Please don't. But she did.

"Did you ever hear the old song 'Grandma's Hands' by Bill Withers?"

"ChrissyJo," I said.

"Yes, Betty?" Her bamboo ear gauges appeared infected at the rim. Her hair was the color of dried mustard.

"Nothing," I said.

I wanted to tell her—like the people say—to keep that man's name out of her mouth, for that was the very moment I knew in earnest that she was an enemy infiltrator, but I bit my tongue. Sometimes, in the end, it's better that way. Just let them do the talking. Truth will out.

It was a strange thing to lie there like that next to her, knowing damn well what was coming. I remember the grass was dry and limp beneath me. I saw a raptor way up high. I watched a stinkbug navigate the tip of my pinky toe while ChrissyJo blathered on.

She soon enough asked a question about the founders of the Fortify Collective, and not long after that, she asked another question, this time about the mythical smelter of Freon Hill. How thoroughly oven-baked this bitch must have been to think I wouldn't smell a rat by then. She went so far as to ask me, "Is it true you're the only one who knows how to run the blast furnace?"

* * *

My pelt tingled. My follicles hummed. I decided to take it all a different direction before I made my move. I turned my head to ChrissyJo and she likewise turned hers to me. She met my eyes with her own and I smiled to her, and winked, and I told ChrissyJo that there was no mythical smelter, and that while I appreciated her prayerful ways, I'd heard enough prayers in my time. I said knuckles was only knuckles, knees nothing but knees. I told her about the big middle bones on Georgie Smythe's fingers when she decapitated beans.

"I don't follow," she said.

I told her I'd made weapons out of bone and teeth. I narrowed my eyes and made my voice like Robert Shaw's in *The Sting*. I said, "You're gonna get yourself a new game. You folla?"

She giggled. Frowned. It is a difficult thing to lie on the ground, shoulder to shoulder in a staredown with a woman like me. Her triceps tensed. Her forearm too. Her hand was getting itchy.

I said: "This isn't your game, ChrissyJo. Even for a lugger, you let out too much rope."

And still she said, "I don't follow." By then her forehead was running sweat. The artery at her temple thumped like a worm.

"ChrissyJo," I said. "I've killed murderous men across three centuries, slavecatchers and rapists and them that harm children, but I ain't never killed no woman."

Poor thing made such a sad quiet sound then.

I told her she had a choice to make. She could reach for her dagger quick and go down in history as the only woman I'd ever put down, or she could reach for it slow and easy, and hand it on over and live to see another tick of the clock. "Keep in mind, honey," I said, "I haven't killed nobody in nineteen years and I aim to make twenty."

She started to speak but could not. She could only swallow the way some folks do when they suddenly fear for their lives. Their mouth goes dry and they cannot produce enough spittle to make a sound. I have always felt sorry for those with such a condition.

A shadow again over the far-off canopy. "Well, would you look at that?" I said. I pointed to the ridgeline where the sun was setting down. A great horned owl soared.

She turned her head to look. I rolled her way, slipping my old hand in quick as a serpent's strike, plucking that knife from its home. I stuck its point to her throat and swung a leg over ChrissyJo, and set my knees on her forearms, and parked my formidable backside on her ribs. In my left fist, I snatched a hank of those dried-out dreads and yanked her head down hard to the dirt. I pressed that knife's tip a little firmer at her carotid.

Her breathing seized up. She didn't even squirm.

I said, "You with the aryans or the Turnbucks?"

Her mouth made a dry sound. She smelled like deer shit. My question was a tricky one, as there was overlap between the two options I'd given.

When she still didn't answer, I pressed harder the point of the blade and broke it through, just a smidge. She spilled it then. Cried an awful lot. She'd married Pinch&Peanut Turnbuck's cousin Carl when he returned from Eastern Europe on a trash tanker in '26 and within a year she was radicalized to the point of this elaborate undercover infiltration. I won't wade into the rest. She claimed she'd changed since coming to the mountain, claimed she saw the truth of humanity now, that she denounced the white boys from which she'd sprung. "I denounce them, Betty!" she kept squealing. It was a sad, leaky affair and I just kept my mouth shut and my wide end parked. My weight had slowed her respiratories quite considerably.

I stood up and she just lay there. I took out my emergency whistle and blew the code of sevens. I could see the barn down below, the red shed. I kept one eye on ChrissyJo, the other on the grounds below. Dot was soon enough at the big steel padlock, turning her key.

I told ChrissyJo she was lucky. "You're a lucky little girl," I said. "I might have killed you right here had I not pledged otherwise to the Theravada Buddhists so long ago."

I could see the line of them coming up the footpath. Dot was in front, strapped into her gat, Rimmy behind her with his old ball bat. If Ancella had still been alive, she'd have squatted on her heels and aimed her Yashica, waiting on a voice that always came and told her when to push the shutter.

We kept ChrissyJo fed and watered and locked and guarded in cabin 6, questioning her now and again about the Turnbucks and the splintered groups of dumbshit white boys and former police still hanging on, still trying to play slave patrol. I generally found ChrissyJo to speak with a liar's tongue, but others heard different, and they believed her when she cried, and they stood at morning meeting and said we ought to find forgiveness in our hearts for the repentant. My niece was one of those. She was still pining away, and I'd made my pledge to quit killing, and so we kept ChrissyJo among the living. And one morning in the spring of '31, she was gone, and we never saw her, nor my niece, again.

I called a special meeting that spring morning when the two of them were gone. I stood on the big sycamore stump before the people of Freon Hill. "You all know where they've gone to," I said. The people milled about and leaned on young trees. I said, "They've gone to Mosestown. They're bearing north on 52 right now, likely pit-stopping at Huntington by midweek."

They didn't want to hear the names of their old beloved cities. It hurt them to hear the names. Two of the little ones ran for the stringbean rows, laughing. Everybody was taking deep breaths. I said, "Don't forget the kind of fire we had here in '24."

It was quiet. They looked at their feet.

I said, "Everybody keep your whistle round your neck."

SONG OF PROVIDENCE

Stanley Knox could purse his lips tight under his nose, and suck, and make a noise to mimic the worm-eating warbler, who called a song more like a bug than a bird. Did you ever hear the song of the worm-eating warbler? You'd think such a sound came from a horny house cricket sawing his legs. The children would tell Stanley, "Do it again!" and he always did.

That first year on the mountain, they'd run to get the basketball and make him crossover and spin and go behind his back on the dirt while they tried to pick his pocket, three on one. They'd blindfold him with a sock and push him further and further back from the barn-door hoop, and they'd roar when he hit those rainbow threes from the pasture fence. Every time the ball hit the net, they jumped up and down hollering catchphrases they'd learned from Stanley, words whose origin was lost to them, "Make It Rain!" they'd shout. "Boom Goes the Dynamite!" "Game, Blouses!"

You wouldn't believe me if I told you of the life and death of Stanley Knox. I don't think I could do it anyway, not fully, not without going to the bad place again. I believe I'll just give you the pieces you need and we'll leave it at that.

When he was a little boy, Auntie Eel used to point at him. "This one here?" she'd say, and she'd hook him by the neck and hug him tight to her pillar of a leg. "He hatched from the egg ain't nobody peppered." She could see Stan was wild. He knew no tribe, and yet he knew every tribe. Always, he brought different folks together by showing them what was the same. When he looked you in the eyes, you wanted to touch him. It was just that way.

But Stanley was on junk full time for three years, from 2008 to 2011. Before that, for eight years, from 1999 through the end of 2007, it was oxys and various other narcotics, and before that and all the way through, from 1989 to 2011, it was drink. Always it was drink. Even through the peak basketball years. You need to understand that. He was not sober when he brought home a state championship at MHS, not sober during his singular year of college ball at Moses U, not sober at his workouts for NBA scouts. He was not sober when the Washington Bullets took him as the thirty-second pick in the 1994 NBA draft, and he was not sober when he averaged 14, 6, and 4 that rookie season, his only one in the association. He finished third in rookie-of-the-year votes behind Jason Kidd and Grant Hill, and then he failed three drug tests in the summer of 1995.

In case you don't know what junk means, it's heroin. In case you don't know what 14, 6, and 4 means, that's a season per-game average: points, assists, and rebounds. A look at his career stats and highlights would tell you he was a six-four shooting guard, and that the release on his jumper was something to behold, that he had quick feet and could get to the tin, that he could defend.

What stats wouldn't tell you is this: his hoops name was Choco-leche, a phrase routinely shouted by the dazzling French color man for SIG Strasbourg during Stan's record-breaking 2001–2 season in France. Most people think this name came from being a light-skinned American player in Spain. The truth is that the nickname was coined by Rigo Rivas in 1999. He'd grown tired of SportsCenter's love affair with Sacramento's Jason Williams—White Chocolate—who hailed from just down the road in Belle.

Basketball gave Stanley so many greats to emulate, but his favor-ite, the one he called the most underrated player in history, was Huntington's own Hal Greer. It's why Stan wore jersey #16 in college and #15 in the pros. Like his father Paul before him, Stan revered Greer. It wasn't only that Mr. 15 Footer was from just downriver, where Paul had watched him play high school ball at Frederick Douglass. It wasn't that his 80 percent free-throw average was achieved by way of a jump shot, and it wasn't his fast break pull-up or his NBA championship with the Sixers. It wasn't even his world-class middle-distance jumper. For Stanley, it was the thigh pad and the lace-up knee brace, and it was what such armor said about the man. Greer was a yeoman of the guards, a ritualist, devout in his attainment of consistency. Stan loved Greer for the look he wore on his face when he played, and for the look he wore on his face when he didn't play. Hal Greer had—as Dot used to say about quiet, expressionless people—worlds in the pupils of his eyes, and he didn't give a damn if you wanted to know what they looked like.

Stanley had worlds inside him, from the pupils of his eyes to the souls of his toes. One of his worlds was basketball, and it took him to D.C. and Spain and France. When his body could take it no more, he flew home to Mosestown, where bad luck and trouble were waiting still. When he went under, he always came back up, for Stan was possessed of a deep and abiding belief in the holy trinity. Mixtape, Barbeque, and Basketball. It was with these three things that he orchestrated all of our lives.

He was locked up at Huttonsville when Memphis died. They didn't grant him a release for the funeral of his only child. That was one time Stanley almost didn't come back up. He only lived because he medicated. Praise be to the unknown gods who make it so easy to cop junk in every choky.

After he got paroled, some folks didn't like the way Stan did his cleaning up, in particular the fact that he never ditched the weed. He doubled down on it instead. He smoked it and vaped it and ate it. He ground its stems into magnificent teas. He took over the land at Freon Hill and cultivated and sold it to his lawn-care customers in impressive increments. Later, he distributed it for free. It's safe to say buckwheat kept Stanley off everything else. From January 2011 until he died in '24, he did not put a drop of alcohol to his lips nor pull a rail of coke. Never swallowed a single oxy nor vike nor perc. No mouthwash. No ibuprofen. With the singular, cannabistic exception, Stan quit everything.

LawnsByKnox kept him in shape. He built a little trailer for his rotary mower and pulled it behind him on his bike. His black beard was as big as Paul Bunyan's and the whole of him was imposing, thick at the chest. He perpetually wore the same thing: a tan LawnsByKnox deerstalker hat and big mirrored safety glasses. Flip flops and football socks, cleats if he was cutting grass, Chuck Taylors otherwise. Plain t-shirt and basketball shorts with a rotted elastic waistband, drawstring yanked out, sagging where his ole walkman rode.

He started LawnsByKnox and mowed 10,000 lawns. He cultivated a high-acreage cannabis crop at Freon Hill and sold 10,000 pounds.

He oversaw the installment of nine city basketball courts. He founded Baton&Bicycle, for he was a DUI repeater and a convicted felon and could own no firearm and drive no car, and as such he found that he preferred bicycles anyway, and weapons you could swing in your fist. Stan thought deep on steel and fuel, and he aimed to put an end to vehicles and firearms. He wrote treatises about water and air and flesh and bone and peace and violence, and he read them with gusto to the Mosestown city council and the board of trustees at Moses U. He bloomed into something magnificent and unforeseen, and then he was gone. He merits, at the very least, a song.

Once upon a time, in March of 2017—before he'd knocked out Peanut Turnbuck on film, before white nationalists began enacting his greatest horror by driving their vehicles over people on the street—he was a guest speaker in Rimmy's special topics writing class at Moses U. It was called *Words That Shake Up the World.* Rimmy had the students reading Studs Terkel and Lucille Clifton and James Baldwin and the like. Stan was in a phase wherein he had immense energy and spirit, a manic optimism preceding his coming August low. I accompanied him to the class.

He was there as an example of thought in action, and he was good. A hometown legend and ex-pro-athlete-ex-con with HARD KNOX tattooed across his knuckles. He looked the students in the eyes and asked them where they were from. He told them that art, food, and sport were the great unifiers; he spoke on community healing through the construction of basketball courts and vegetable gardens with large-scale muraled walls. He told them about the children Bob Moses led, about standing on the streetcorner and bouncing a ball, for if you bounce it, they will come. He told them about the Algebra Project and said to them, "You all are writers. What if there was a writing project the likes of the Algebra Project and you took it into the local schools?" He said to them, "What if we proclaimed that our fine city was named not for a greedy capitalist Moses but instead a people's hero Moses? Imagination plus work can make anything be."

A young man who sat in the front scoffed. Stan paused, looked at him, then continued.

The young man in question was small and pale and the beds of his fingernails were faintly blue. Rimmy had told us about him. In his critical responses to assigned readings, he'd been increasingly expressing himself as a white supremacist. I'll never understand why that boy chose that particular day to say something aloud. I'll exist in wonderment over how someone could be around Stanley Knox and test him in that manner.

Stan was saying something about taking the people to the street when the young man made what he likely believed was a joke. Something about "libtards" being run over. Stan found nothing funny in it. He invited the young man to join him outside, three times, like this: "Come on, let's just step outside together for a minute and talk," and when the young man thrice declined his invitation, Stan gathered him up lickety-split in a fireman's carry and took him to the green round of grass out front of the bell-towered building, and there he set the young man on an aluminum bench and bent to him, forehead to forehead with his hands on his knees, and he spoke quietly to the pale shook child, words that would no doubt right many a young man's ship, but not this one. This one's father filed a complaint with the university and hired a lawyer.

One of the other students had gotten her phone recording just as Stan exploded into a precise lightning strike, a blur that resulted in the fireman's carry. The video was used as evidence by the complainant. It is mostly just shaky footage taken through a window, looking out at the green. The audio consists of chair-leg scrapes against the floor and someone saying again and again, "Oh, shit." Someone else says, "Yall know he had it comin." Rimmy is heard to audibly concur with this assessment. At the evidentiary hearing, the complainant's lawyer cranked the volume and everyone went quiet. She played it twice, unmistakably Rimmy's cadence and timbre.

> Student: Yall know he had it comin.
> *Chair-leg scrape.*
> Professor: A fool come to judgment.

When questioned, Rimmy stood by this remark throughout the proceedings. He stood by it until the end.

In the final hearing, Rimmy gave a statement before the scant representatives of the faculty senate and the scant representatives of legal affairs and student services and human resources and the provost's office. He'd written the statement that morning, in a moment of beautiful clarity, on the back of a flier for window tinting. He read it to them.

"The rightwing fundamentalist white extremists have brought their sleight of hand inside the academic bubble, and you all are nothing more than marks, lollygagging at their flimsy card table. You used to have book smarts and now you have screen smarts, but your eyes and ears were never practiced at life. In this case, you are on record for citing the First Amendment, again and again. Now I am on record pointing out that you have taken the side of a racist with a funny bone for vehicular murder."

They could not look at him. Not a one.

He went off script. "I want you to see yourselves for who you are," he said, and he spoke of the koch brothers' donations to the business school and he spoke of the invited lecture of little jimmy vance, a snake-oil man of the Estabrook-Davenport persuasion. "What was the speaker's fee on that one?" he asked them, and when he was met with silence, he answered his own question. "I believe it was fifty large." He pointed out that this was more than his annual salary. "Five figures," he said, "for an hour of flyblown horse shit."

He raised his voice. "My brother's name hangs on a banner from the rafters of your coliseum, and now you've banned him from your grounds? For doing what any parent would do if their child was killed in a hit-and-run?"

He was met with more silence, and then thanked for his testimony, and after that, in short order, he was relieved of his job.

That was when Rimmy turned from writing to the visual arts, and that was the true start of our mobilizing times. Underneath the silence of those university people I heard something faint but rising. A scream, a shriek, a door sprung open. The sound their silence tried to cover is what called forth our roar and chalked our bullhorn course to the civic center and, later, out into the choked thoroughfares, our signs held high and our masks on tight, the song of Bill Withers in our ear. The sound their silence tried to cover was the sound of Magnolia and Georgie Smythe and every other held down chopped down strung up and buried brother and sister and cousin and grandbaby I ever knew and loved. The sound came out on the paper inside *The Fortify Collective Guide to Resistance.* I only wish it hadn't all gone to my head and put me on a floatplane to Mykonos.

Nearly every FCGR was burned in '24, and I don't believe my roar will ever be what it was, but all my years of living with people like the Knoxes of Mosestown have taught me one thing for certain.

I will never bend an ear to the authors of our misery.

SONG OF RECURRING DREAM
#77

Rimmy Knox opens and closes his mouth but no sound emerges. His teeth are silver-gilded. They are jutted in the extreme and they are close upon me, opening and closing slow and silent but for breathing. I put up a hand to shield myself and note that my fingers, at middle knuckle, angle hard right. I raise my left hand and it is the same. I mean to say that the fingers are sharply, crudely, uniformly bent. My thumbs are angled as they always have been, but from each has sprouted a second, smaller thumb that waggles in unison with its loco parentis.

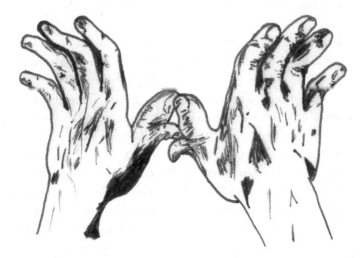

"Rimmy," I say. "Rimmy, look at this here."

But when I raise my eyes, he's gone. In his place, it's the old mute rag man, and at his side is not a chair but a white iron cooler filled with green glass bottles of Coca-Cola nestled into mountainous peaks of machine-cut ice, the bottles tilted just so, like dildos in their clear acrylic stands. The rag man's rags are smoldering and fluttering away like a leaf-pile fire. He bangs on the cooler's side with his whale-dong walking cane. "Car wash!" he yells in the voice of a child. "Fundraiser! Secret tunnel!"

I say to him, "You can talk now?" but this makes him cry straight-away and he takes off like a shot. I long to give chase but I cannot move. I look down. I am buried to the waist in dirt. There are crick-ets covering the ground, hopping every which way but loose, not a chirp to be heard, the world so quiet you could hear a pube drop.

Then I waggle my ears and work my jaw side to side and I begin to hear it, quiet but coming louder.

I hear the song of the undulating bugs.

SONG OF THE FLOOD

The last time I saw her among the living, Eloise Baach put on quite a show. She wasn't holding back at age ninety-two. It was a fine display of some of her greatest hits and choicest cuts. She must have said "You're full a mud" six times that day. Didn't put her teeth in the whole time. "You hungry?" she kept asking us, "cause I got two knuckle sandwiches right here."

Everybody called her Auntie Eel, even if she wasn't their kin. She was Ancella's half-sister, and when the big storm came, Ancella asked us to go over to Eel's trailer on Sharp Creek and force her to vacate. Ancella had already tried herself, but to no avail. I'd been to that big trailer so many times over the years and, every time, I stood out back and looked at the creek's switchback, and thought of Magnolia.

Eel might listen to me, or if not me then Dot, or if not Dot then Rimmy, or if not Rimmy then surely Stanley. Everybody listened to Stanley.

It was the first Saturday in March of '23, the day after my birthday. I'd told everyone I was eighty-eight that year, watched their puzzled faces, heard their refrains, "Betty, you just don't age." The ones who knew, knew.

I remember I could feel the water coming. I could feel it in my knuckles and in my knees. By 8:00 that morning, the meteorologist was saying "stalled front" and "boundary," much like he had in June 2016. Everybody got on the horn. Dot's truck had the highest clearance. She picked me up and we grabbed Stan and Rimmy by 10:00. We hit the Tudor's drive-thru and rolled up to Eel's at 10:30.

* * *

Her yard was wet as a sponge. The creek, just behind her trailer, was already over its banks. I couldn't even see Magnolia's switchback. The neighbor couple tore off their property on a four-wheeler. I knew they were tough women. That morning they wore ski goggles and raincoats, and they waved to us, duffle bags and rifles slung on every shoulder.

Eel's signage had gone crooked in the yard. Its paint needed a touch-up. Purple sky, big yellow sun: *Fortune Teller Auntie Eel, Tea Leaves & Tarot.*

Dot had to knock five or six times before Eel opened up. She wore silk-embroidered house slippers and a robe she'd stolen from the Greenbrier. She told us we might as well come in out of the rain. "But I ain't leavin," she said. "I'll tell you that right now."

The doormat was oversized and read *SHAZBOT!* We tried to shake off the rain. The place smelled like fried eggs and high-grade buckwheat and the finest sandalwood incense money could buy. Sam Cooke and the Soul Stirrers on the hifi, singing "Peace in the Valley." Eel walked away from us toward the kitchen. "Yall hungry?" she asked, then mumbled to herself about the knuckle sandwiches.

"Got Tudor's on the way over," Dot said. "There's a hot Peppi waiting on you in the car." Her voice was always pitched high when she was nervous.

Rimmy said, "You ride shotgun, Eel, that goes without saying."

She stopped and turned around to face us from across the room. It was suddenly quiet. "Peace in the Valley" had ended, and here came "Lord Remember Me." Our little ship was tossed and driven.

* * *

Stanley was feeling what I was about the flood, in the blood and bone. He said, "Listen. The water is coming. It's already washed out Portsmouth and if it keeps on like it is, it'll wash out everything on the creek by noon."

"You're full a mud," Eel said. She sat down in a high-back toile chair that once was brown and white. She gripped her homemade leather cigarette case. It was of the coin-purse variety. When she closed it, the little offset silver snap made a pleasing sound. She opened it and snapped it shut again. She regarded us.

"Only thing I'm full of," Stan said, "is utmost certainty."

Eel lit up her Tareyton Long and laughed in a genuine fashion. "You employ the word *utmost* these days, do you, Stanley?" She winked at me. Gray roots grew like ice from the part in her hair.

Stan said, "I employ a great many things these days, Eloise," and wasn't that the truth. Nobody could deny Stanley his range of ceaseless physical and intellectual motion. He'd foretold the big storm and the flood and the coming war and disarmament. I suspect he'd seen his own coming death by then. His intuition and his vision had far surpassed that of Eel, and she knew it like the rest of us did, but she was the fortuneteller by trade, not he. She was ninety-two to his fifty-one. It was her home we stood in, not his. It was her place of business, her purple batik moonglow, her incensed air wafting a glorious vegetative bloom in back where the stalks of sinsemilla grew beneath the timed and gentle lights, the sprinkling waters.

Stan cleared his throat. He was shifting his weight from one foot to the other. The sidewalls of his low-top All Stars were clean as a whistle though we'd just stepped through a glade.

* * *

"Utmost my thumb," Eel said. "Can't nobody know the rain." She pulled a tub of chocolate pudding from the mini-fridge beside her chair, peeled the flimsy top off, and licked it.

"Eel, please come with us," Dot said.

"Mmmmmm," the old woman said. "Any of you ladies and gentlemen care for chocolate jello pudding?" She licked the top again and smiled at us, toothless. She said, "You can't be a kid without it." Before we could answer in the affirmative, as we always had, she threw the opened tub at Stan's head. He managed to duck and the pudding hit a framed black-and-white photograph of Dizzy Gillespie hung by the door. Eel had taken it at the Theatrical Grill in Cleveland in February of 1966. Later, on the girl's twentieth birthday, Eel gave that camera to Ancella Baach and, in doing so, chalked forever her course.

Eel said, "I wasn't hungry anyway," and regarded her cigarette where it smoldered in the green glass ashtray beside her. She fiddled with her pouch. I shut my eyes and listened for the snap to close. "Utmost my ass," I heard her say again, this time very quietly. The old black rotary phone on the wall began to ring, but no one moved. No one said a word. After six rings, it stopped.

Stanley shifted his weight. Dot stepped off the Shazbot mat but Eel raised a hand, told to her to wait until every drop was dripped. "And in this house," she went on, "we wear house shoes, and if you have neglected to remember your own, a pair can be made available to you for a double sawbuck."

My knees ached. Rimmy cleared his throat and started to speak, but didn't.

* * *

Eel mumbled, "Fig-head comin in here calling me by my full first name like we contemporaries." She raised her voice. "Don't call me no Eloise! You call me Eel or Auntie Eel like every other pauper on my walk!" She took hold of the old chair's threadbare paws and resituated herself. I could tell by the way she regarded Dizzy Gillespie that she regretted her temper's steam. It wasn't the first time.

We could feel her coming around. We side-eyed one another, and we knew if we kept our mouths shut, she might budge.

The kangaroo pouch on the front of the cigarette case bore her debossed initials: EBB. Eloise Brandywine Baach. If somebody was around who didn't know her, and that somebody said, "What does EBB stand for," Eel would blow smoke at their face and answer—without missing a beat—in one of two ways. If she'd sized the stranger up as dumb: "Every Body's Business, honey. That's my line a work, and business been good." If she'd sized the stranger up as smart: "Doesn't stand for anything, honey. It's a word. Ebb. As in the ebb and flow of life's current. Don't you get that station?"

That's where she kept her traveling fortunes, the little pouch on the front of her cigarette case. By that day in March of 2023, Eel had composed, laminated, and disseminated 9,000 traveling fortunes, by my rough estimate. To be clear, these were not wholesale conventional fortunes. Eel wrote these fortunes in a book, in pencil, and later, she typed them on her typewriter, and ran a sheet of forty unique phrases through her hand-crank lamination machine, and then cut them on a guillotine paper cutter that screamed every time she brought down the cast-iron arm.

I lost so many of those fortunes over the years. They said things like:

The catfish has the eyes of the fisherman who hooks him.
Listen to the wisdom of the dead.
The cherry is made of wine.

I managed to hang on to my favorite. I keep it in my brassiere.

Lamb has got to bleat, and Lion has got to roar.

Stanley looked back at Dizzy Gillespie, frozen black and white by Eel's old Yashica. Dizzy had been in the grips of a big blow, his magnificent neck threatening the seams of his shirt collar. Pudding slid down his black jacket lapel slick as a slug trail. Stanley looked at me. He took off his ball cap. The skin on his fingers was pink from laserbeam tattoo removal. He looked at Eel. He said, "Please."

She let go her grip of the armrests and picked up her cigarette. "Yall kids get the fuck out and me and Betty will gather my valuables and she'll drive me in the Oldsmobile."

I nodded my head.

"Done," Dot said, and they opened the door to leave.

Stanley told us to hurry.

When we heard the truck backing out, Eel sighed and opened her robe and rubbed her kneecaps in a circular fashion. "How much longer we got to go on like this?" she asked me.

I said I'd start packing.

"Give me just one moment," Eel said. She leaned again to the mini-fridge and this time took out a tub of VapoRub. She scraped a hunk of balm from the bottom, and in the same circular fashion, she worked it into her knees and shins and calves.

I went to the kitchen. Out the tall windows, the creek had come up in the yard. We were short on time. I stood and beheld the mess. Next to a stack of egg-yolked plates was a standing roll of $100 notes, rubberbanded and big around as a ball bat. I picked it up, stepped back into the living room, and handed it to Eel. "Wouldn't want to forget that," I said.

"It's a fortune all for you," she said, and she smiled a little bit and stuck it into the pocket of her robe. I asked if she wanted me to pack the kitchen china. "No," she said. "Flower first and foremost. Go to my bathroom and start clippin buds."

She seemed stuck in her chair. There was residual VapoRub on her fingers. She wiped it inside her nose and inhaled, put away the balm, sighed again, and regarded her swollen old ankles. The elastic in her house slippers was overly constrictive. There were

tissues stuffed in the toes. Sam Cooke kept right on singing that
the water was not in the well.

Before I went back to clip buds, the wall phone started ringing
again, and after the first ring, Eel stood and went to the kitchen
and returned with a steel meat mallet. She raised it up and brought
it down hard on the telephone—significantly more power left in
her than I'd have guessed—and the ring sound briefly went silly,
like a tiny calliope had fired up inside. The plastic cracked as only
1970s plastic can, and the phone dropped from the wall, slack black
cord whip-cracking straight, phone swinging like a dead man.

Eel set the mallet on the TV cabinet and smiled. She said to me, "Do
you know that phone hadn't rung more than once a year before those
two just now?" She laughed and so did I. "Let's get to packin," she said.

The rain picked up and beat the roof so hard we had to holler just
to hear each other speak. We'd gotten most everything cinched in
garbage bags by the time the water topped the trailer's foundation.
I'd been waiting for a break in the downpour to go out and start
the Oldsmobile. Eel had put on galoshes and a rain hat.

The trailer groaned. We looked out front again. The water was at
the windowsill. I didn't think we'd be able to open the door.

"Lord," Eel said. "Let's go look out the back." And so we walked to
the kitchen together, and we looked out the big windows, watched
the water climb halfway up the panes.

Eel laughed a little bit again. "We're fish in a tank," she said.

"We're in a fine kettle a fish," I answered.

* * *

"More like kettle a shit." And we were too stunned to laugh by then. We just stood and stared. Eel said, "Look at that. Might as well be Ovaltine, brown as it is." Sharp Creek was a wide raging river now. Its waves lashed the windows all the way to the top. Every seam in the place squealed.

A ten-foot basketball goal spun close, wild in the current. A collapsed corrugated shed.

I could not believe what I was seeing. I've witnessed water rise fast and take out a concrete bridge. I've seen a river come over its banks and pick up a crop tractor like a tin can. I've seen flash floods and river bursts all my life, but I've never seen speed or power like that day. I said, "Eel, I don't know that there's much we can do but I think we ought to make a plan." And she reached out then, and took my hand.

She remarked on the basketball goal caught and spinning in the current. "I know that hoop," she said, a strange confusion set in her brow. "Belongs to a little skinny boy down at Pea Cut." The kitchen windows exploded and brown-white water burst through the opening in a perfect square column, knocking Eel into me and covering us up in an instant. My tailbone cracked a low cabinet door. The kitchen was a splintercat. I tumbled heels over head, forks and knives darting betwixt downspouts and tree roots, aluminum siding gone inside out. What a churn. What a thrashing ordeal it had instantly become.

I had Eel in my grasp for a moment. My fingers raked her ribcage, pawed the slick sheen of her VapoRub legs, and then she was gone, and then it was quiet and black.

* * *

Eel was one of forty-eight people to die that day in Mosestown.
Fifty more up and down the Ohio and its tributaries.

When they asked me about it afterward, I said I couldn't remember.
I said I'd hit my head. I told no one how I'd come to clutching a
high branch in a pignut hickory tree, five miles downriver from
Eel's, all that water still chopping beneath me. In a nearby branch,
a big stand-up bass had been snagged by a thick waving limb.
It hung there by the top string. I could hear the wind whistle
through its f-holes.

There was not one stitch of clothing left on me. I was naked as a
jaybird once again, this time wrapped around a tree branch.

The rain had quit, and when the water finally receded, I climbed
down. All around me, as far as I could see, were more trees. Some
stood and some lay on their side. I walked barefoot in the deep
black mud. Night fell. Little light of moon, dark and quiet as the
old days.

Later on that night, I was sidestepping a shattered red spruce when
I heard one single sound. It was Eel's hifi playing again, and though
it came in an echo from way up the ridge, Sam Cooke was clear
as a bell. He sang to me, "Mighty lion, you will lie down with the
lamb." I hummed along. I walked through the night.

I am walking still.

SONG OF THE OXHERD

There once was a meditation hall in the deep forest of Hampshire County, and its walls and ceiling were paneled in reclaimed oak, a pleasing light finish with dark knots aplenty. December 3, 2010, was a cloudless Friday, and I stood in that meditation hall for a silent afternoon session, while all around me the others sat on their knees. My own knees ached too much for that kind of bending. I'd been given permission by Bhante Gunaratana to stand.

This wasn't my first rodeo at Bhavana. Ancella knew Bhante G personally, and over the years, he'd let me come stay a week here and there, when I'd gone to the bad place again. This time was different. Darker. Memphis was freshly gone. I'd killed the boy that hit her on Dug Hill Road. I was fit to explode, and something had to give.

Around me, a dozen human animals breathed with much volume and force. Windowpane sunlight warmed my shut eyelids, a moving fiery wall. The bad place was as bad as it had ever been. The ringing in my ears was thereminic, the roaring in my skull full-throated. Somebody's foot odor was exceptionally pungent. A fly alighted on my brow but I could not smack it.

The woman to my left audibly farted, and I instantly thought of my smiling grandbaby, eating her car-seat cheerio in the rearview in August, her eyes knowing all that they knew. I suppose there was something in the particular resonance and texture of the meditating woman's fart that made it strike me as it did but, whatever the case, my ear ringing instantly quit and my skull went soft and empty like a mud-dauber nest. I heard the unmistakable voice of Memphis Knox yet again, but this time she spoke a lovely tongue I'd never understand. I opened my eyes. The massive triangular window behind the altar buddha had become the sunlight's portal, carrying a brilliant column of rays into us all like floodwater through an exploded pane. So bright was its light that every human animal before its glow was a shadow, a lackluster eclipse. Every breath was an echo of an old, old breath. I kept my eyes open. I saw no fishbirds on the column of light. I heard no *thip sup*. This was an altogether different vision.

The altar buddha was a melting silhouette, rags smoldering. The arched windows lining the sidewalls opened inward like beaks and hummed a tune I knew but couldn't place. The vaulted ceiling was the upturned hull of a glass-bottom boat, but instead of sky it revealed twelve tops of twelve concrete footings, and six steel columns, and a web of rebar and a nest of wax-paper hamburger wrappers, yellow as the sun. In between, there was dirt. I saw worms the size of rat snakes up there, sidewinding, wringing themselves out. And then they were still, and the whole ordeal became a fixed cathedral painting, muted and dull, every grain of silt a star, every length of iron a tree branch. I dropped to my knees but felt no pain.

I'm not able to put into words what happened to me inside the sun's rays that day in the meditation hall. But I knew I was once again free from the bad place, and the people and things around were effigies and chimes, and their hummed refrain was a recoiling helix to the sun, unending. I knew I would someday soon be untamed on a hill where there were no vehicles or guns or cops, and Black and brown people could be free, and I could pull off my clothes and move about in the world as I saw fit and use the bathroom where and when I pleased, and lie down on my back and stretch, and look up at the sky. I knew I would not have to take any more lives. I would only have to save them.

* * *

You must believe me: I had not planned to kill that Turnbuck boy. I didn't sharpen my blade nor feed sugarcubes to any tied horses. Had Pinch Turnbuck not been the son of a cop, had he not posted bail, had I not gone to his mandatory AA meeting and sat in the back with my hood up, had I not seen him laughing there with his buddy who sported nazi SS bolts on his neck and slipped Pinch an oxy right in the church basement, ankle monitor badges on their gym socks, had I not caught him pulling into his lot at 4 a.m. all alone, piloting his daddy's Escalade, drunk behind the wheel on Thanksgiving, had he not told me—when I stepped out of the shadow of the rhododendron and asked him what he thought he was doing—"Fuck off, you fat cunt," had none of that happened, then maybe I wouldn't have pinned him to the blacktop by his throat and squeezed and squeezed, and told him what I knew about life and steel and death.

It was a long and quiet speech. The whites of his eyes swelled and turned red as two blood moons. I put him down a mineshaft no one knows about but me.

All that fell away on December 3 inside the mediation hall, and I didn't protest that night when one of the monastics found me leaning on a willow tree outside the dining hall and said he was the bearer of bad news. I remember I was picking my teeth with a matchbook and told him he need not worry, I had not smuggled in cigarettes or beef jerky this time around.

"I believe you, Betty," he said over his glasses. I can't recall his name, but he was the only white monastic on the place, a kind bald man. "But I'm sorry to say that someone has reported that you brought in marijuana in the form of banana bread."

I told him I liked his phrasing of things. And he was right. The floral stank wafting off the little half-loaf was overpowering, even if I only opened the jar for a couple of seconds. I'd seen the farting woman take a hard sniff of air when I'd pinched a chunk off at dinner. She had the look of a snitch. A note-taking, farting snitch on corporate retreat. If I had a nickel for every one of them I've met.

"You know the policy, Betty." He pushed up the bridge of his glasses. His robe was in serious need of washing. "No substances."

I told ole what's-his-name to rest easy. I was feeling all better after the sunbeam vision, and beyond that, I knew he'd arrange a ride for me, at least to the Citgo four miles north on Route 50, and there I could procure cigarettes, and that is truly something to look forward to in this life. I had a new spring in my step. I hugged the monastic man tight and said I'd pack my things.

And after that, I never killed nobody again.

SONG OF RECURRING DREAM
#99

Used to be I was walking a narrow path through limestone high-walls, wet fallen logs here and there, moss on every last one. I followed a woman I could not make out. She was tall with sharp shoulders. Barefoot. We never found our destination. Sometime in 2011, the woman was suddenly a man, and I followed him through ill-lit musty hallways, always to nowhere, always without a face or a voice. The man became Stanley in '24 and stayed that way, and he began to speak to me at such length and with such startling clarity that I had to make another dream journal just to fit it all in.

In the dream I follow Stanley down a narrow corridor in the upper stacks of the Moses U main library. He talks while he walks, reciting passages from the speeches he gave at all those city council meetings.

"The arterial highway of the human animal is much too close to the pelt," he says. "The active human's musculature may in some cases act as a partial barrier to exterior metals, whether a knife or an aluminum guardrail."

I smell a familiar scorched oil. It emanates from somewhere in the ceiling, or it could be the floor.

Stan walks and talks so fast I can hardly keep up. "Any metal traveling at an inhuman rate of speed—whether that metal is two tons or fifty grams—spells trouble for arteries and vessels and organs, particularly if that metal is arriving with such velocity that it's broken the god-damn sound barrier." He drinks from a hole in the coconut he carries.

He stops at a stack of old hardcovers and faces me up and says, "Listen to the sound of your hogleg's retort. That crack on the end is supersonic." He smiles his glorious smile beneath the beard. He taps his coconut and says, "This is the way to rethink flesh and bone."

A phone rings. Stanley takes a hardcover book from the shelf and opens it.

Inside is an old black rotary dial.

Stan lifts the receiver and puts it to his ear. I can hear the people on the other end. They are whispering in an unknown tongue. They are sneezing. "Bless you," Stan says and hangs up.

The ringing has not ceased. Stan says, "That ain't the one, chief," and he pulls from his watch-fob pocket another phone, and he hands it to me. "Don't forget to answer your burner, Betty," he says.

And I slide the little phone inside a watch-fob pocket all my own.

Stan pulls another book from the shelf, and another and another. The pages are all printed backward and upside down. He ascertains them as such and throws them on the ground. I ask him what he's looking for but he does not answer. He litters the floor with unwieldy hardcovers. They knock against one another at our feet like timber in a log dump. "Just don't step on any atlases," he says.

I can't see my feet. There is a droning from beneath the books, like a hollow tree swarming with bees.

Stan says, "Here it is!" He hands me an open book and tells me to read. "This is the one I called your burner about, to sing it to you," he says. "Remember, back when I was dead? Back when I was so little?"

How many times have I read those words in their fearful shape on that old yellowed page? How many times have I finished reading and looked up to find Stanley there before me, his lip trembling, telling me "It'll be okay, it'll be okay." He says, "Listen, I'd always known. Just read it one more time, and then let's go home." And I look down to read it again, but the page is always empty the second time.

Still, I remember that poem plain as day. I remember its edge and its pith, the ore of its sound, the grafted touch of its letters one against the next. I can pen it in under a minute. I can recite it whilst sleepwalking, tongue-tied in a knot.

Woodcutters!
Sleep the morning dry,
And stand on what you reap.
The stuffing in your britches is straw.
The down in your tick is a cotton ball.
The fuel in your tubes is fire,
And the godchild roasts
In the buckwheat
On a pyre.

I have read those words a hundred times or more.

SONG OF THE BUCKETMOUTH
OF TALEPACKIA

The BucketMouth of TalePackia can be whoever you say they are. They can hail from wherever it is you hail. New Orleans, Baltimore, Nome, Port Harcourt, Damascus, Karachi, Yokohama. Like the people say, it don't matter. BucketMouth live all over, but there has always seemed to me, demographically speaking, a high concentration in two particular places. One of those places comprises half the land mass in Mingo and McDowell counties, in southern West Virginia. The other place is Mosestown.

You already know the Knoxes of Mosestown, there pon yon wall. I'd wager—pound for pound—they packed more tales than just about any.

I have already pledged my intent to show you every picture.

I remember when I first asked Paul, here with his Chesterfield clinched and his catfish still swinging, how the children got their names.

"Flipped a nickel," he said.

Turns out this was only true in the case of Stanley, their thirdborn. In 1969, Ancella named their firstborn Dot (Dorothea Lange Knox), after her favorite photographer. In 1972, Paulie named their secondborn Rimmy (Rimfire Hamrick Knox), after his favorite West Virginian. Their third would be their last, and when he was delivered and rolled beneath a heat lamp, Ancella winced in pain as she took a quarter from her hand-knitted cigarette case and said: "Call it in the air." She thumb-flipped it so high it whispered to the ceiling, and she smacked it down on the sunbeaten skin of her opposite hand.

* * *

Paul called tails.

Ancella lifted her hand.

It was tails.

"Stanley," Paul said. "After the thermos I carried seven years fore they took it." Paul never would shut up about how those police took his lucky thermos and never gave it back.

He'd bought it, the green vacuum-top model, in 1968. They were living in Dade County, Florida, back then. Schoolteachers. There was a statewide strike and Paul carried his coffee by the steel handle every morning to the picket line. They lost their jobs and moved back to West Virginia. Seven years later, in May of 1975, Paul came out of his Moses University office and saw, in a parking lot across 3rd Avenue, a man berating a woman. The man hit the woman with a closed fist and Paul ran through traffic across all four lanes, gripping that steel handle, cocking the Stanley as he came, swinging with such precision timing on arrival as to slam the broadside of the thermos into the man's cheek and temple. That man got up off the ground only when the arresting officer lifted him by the cuffs. The thermos was taken by that officer as evidence, never to be seen again.

The cuffed man had six warrants out on things like passing bad checks and possession of methamphetamine. The woman he'd punched was Barbara Ailes. She owned a printing company on 6th Avenue that specialized in large-scale banners. She'd never even met her attacker before that evening at the bar, where he'd insisted that she was someone named Cheryl Bonecutter, a name he'd kept hollering over the music, inadvertently spitting in her face as he told her, "I know you're Cheryl Bonecutter!" It was a memorable name that we later tracked down in a Wayne County phonebook. Barbara Ailes called her up. Sure enough, Cheryl Bonecutter was a woman in Wayne who, in the ninth grade, had cut off all that man's pubic hair after he'd drunk two bottles of Thunderbird and passed out on in the League 3 visitors' dugout. The man had hissed a version of all this in Barbara Ailes's ear at bar's end, where he'd cornered her in front of the garnish tubs. "How you think that made me feel," he'd asked her, "waking up bushwhacked with my briefs at my knees?" When he'd leaned in to order two tequilas, she'd cut out the side door. He'd given chase.

From the time the man exited the tavern door, it was less than a minute to when Paul let him have it with the big Stanley thermos. "Read the police report if you don't believe me," Paul would say.

And that was how we came to know Barbara Ailes. She was okay except for a bloody nose and two teeth she said felt looser than before.

Barbara designed beautiful banners. Her shop made every sign the Fortify Collective ever held high above our heads. No Justice No Peace, Hope Dies Last, Black Lives Matter, Say Her Name. Barbara

Ailes printed the very first *Fortify Collective Guide to Resistance*. Two-color staple-bound. She printed the signs for LawnsByKnox. She printed all the literature for Stanley's citywide public safety initiative to rid ourselves of vehicles and guns, Bicycle&Baton.

Once upon a time in 2019, over the course of five months, Barbara Ailes built a gigantic custom sign on heavy black burlap, thirty-six panels, each one stitched to the next. One to two letters painted on almost every panel, each letter lotus white and standing six feet by three. It could fold and roll and fit in the van. It could be hung by night over the top of a billboard on a primary arterial road. It could be hung by day on the brick face of an apartment building by way of the roof or by neighborly windowpane, and it could always be surveilled and snatched away before the fuzz showed up, and we could always live to fight another day.

It was nearly forty feet tall. Twenty across. We called it the Biggun.

When the president came back to West Virginia in summer 2019, this time to Wheeling, Barbara Ailes and her sign-making crew had set up a week in advance. A metal-sculptor friend of Rimmy's lived in the sixth-floor loft apartment above the old restaurant-supply warehouse on 14th Street, right across from WesBanco Arena, home of the Nailers. WesBanco Arena had once been called the Civic Center, and it was the site of the president's closed-door-coal-baron fundraiser, emceed by little jimmy justice.

Barbara and her crew had long since rolled the Biggun up in a tight column and mounted it over the apartment's long industrial windows. It looked like a put-away awning, like it had always been there. The secret service didn't give it a thought when they cleared the building and the block that morning in July. They could not have known that the awning's magnetic clasps were controlled by a wireless remote transmitter and receiver, crafted by Rimmy's sculptor friend, and as the president exited his vehicle on 14th Street—his admirers shouting on one side of the jersey curb, his detractors shouting on the other—Barbara Ailes and her compatriots sat comfortably down the block in an air-conditioned coffee shop, watching through the clean glass pane. The president's car door shut behind him, and he looked about, and waved.

Barbara pressed the little black button, and the clasps broke free, and the Biggun unrolled like a magic carpet against the bricks and the rows of green glass. It made a notable sound on the wind, not unlike the snap of a sail or the flap of a great horned owl, and its weighted bottom yanked the slack, and all the people in the street below, including the president, craned their necks and shielded their eyes against the sun to read the Biggun's words. And there were discernable moans and cackles, and shouts of joy, and much howling at the sun. They say the president's face flushed from blood orange to only blood. They say he sharted in his adult-diapered carriage, that you could smell it like meconium on the wind as it rose and wafted off the Ohio's choppy roll.

little
donnie
trump
is a
milk-livered
racist devil

I hope you'll appreciate Barbara's choice of words, and maybe you'll roar, and put a fist in the air.

I am trying to choose the songs I believe you'd want to hear.

SONG OF SORROW

I will tell you what happened to Stanley Knox on November 5, 2024. I have pieced it together from the mouths of many, and I've written it down a hundred times or more. Some of it I've likely gotten wrong, but one thing I am certain of is that Stan saw it coming, and he walked to his death with his head held high.

It was election day, at least for those of us who still believed in that kind of thing. For the white nationalists who came out of their holes and into our streets that morning, it was an altogether different kind of day. We knew they would come; we just didn't know it would be like it was.

Stan had breakfast at Shoeless Joe's. Rigo Rivas told me later that Stan sat in his corner booth, regular spot, but he was alone, and quiet, and he ordered double liver and gizzards though he'd not eaten meat in five years. Rigo said he ate every bite and sopped the plate with his biscuit, and they stepped out the side door for a smoke in Memphis's garden, and Stan stared at the brick mural for twenty minutes. Before he left, he hugged Rigo and told him he loved him.

Now Stanley was known to tell people that he loved them, particularly in those times, but everyone I talked to about that day said the same things. *Quiet, tired, said I love you.*

He tried to call me on the burner but I wasn't in range.

Most of us had long since left the city by then. We were building cabins and barns and gardens and ball fields, living full time at Freon Hill. Only Stan and Dot remained in Mosestown, and neither of them spent much time there. Most nights they were with us, and both were set to move to the mountain full time, their leases up in December.

The last one to see him was Dot. He stopped by the apartment and they sat in the window sun and drank coffee. She told me Fat Lever wouldn't leave Stanley alone, circling his feet and sitting on his lap, purring and purring and making those biscuits.

Stan had a delivery to make in Huntington that afternoon. Dot told him not to go, but there was an old woman he knew who lived on 10th Street and she needed him. She'd been his kindergarten teacher, Albert's too. She wanted one of his retooled rotary mowers in order to cut her little patch of grass. She had colon cancer and required an ounce of ChewbaccaPajamas, a new strain he'd grown that fall that whipped the ass of chronic pain and increased one's appetite for whole fruits and vegetables. The old woman said he left her place before 1 p.m.

I figure they got him somewhere between 12th Street and Hal Greer Boulevard, and this pains me in particular, for of all Stan's basketball gods, Hal Greer was whom he loved most.

The white terrorists had selected the neighborhood between 12th Street and Hal Greer Boulevard because that's where the most Black folks lived. The polling place was in the Carter G. Woodson Community Center and, in turn, that's where the terrorists strolled, their pistol grips peeking from their waistbands, not a police in earshot. A little girl I spoke to said she'd seen a man with a big beard get dragged into a silver minivan.

* * *

He'd taken a cab from Mosestown, but the old woman said he'd walked away from her place. "Sun was out," she said. "Nice day for a walk."

What glee they must have felt when they realized it was Stanley walking alone on that broken sidewalk. They'd warned him not to step foot in Huntington again. In the West End and increasingly the East, the white gangs staked a wide turf for hawking their inferior weed. City leadership had flipped in the interim elections two years prior. The police were infiltrated by that time too, back to cracking skulls and slipping cash inside their socks. Chit Turnbuck was their new chief. I knew how much he hated all us Knoxes and Baaches, how he'd blamed Stan for the disappearance of his sons. I knew he'd railed against Baton&Bicycle when a whiff of it came Huntington's way.

I knew that just like his ancestors before him, Chit Turnbuck had dead empty eyes and vacuous blood, the kind of man who whistled and spat and skipped rocks on the water while around him people crumpled and died.

I'm certain it was him who destroyed evidence after that day, who made all their culpability go away. For all I know, he could have stopped them. He could have kept us all from seeing what we saw. But that was their point—for us to see what we saw—and they made it on election day, in a fashion that no one could ever forget.

We awoke on the mountain at four the next morning to the smell and heat of a blazing fire. Up and down every row and all around the harvested field of buckwheat, they'd soaked lines of gasoline and transmission fluid, slow burn to fast for their getaway. By the time we ran from our unfinished cabins, the whole stretch was so bright you had to squint your eyes, so hot you had to stop and take a step back.

Between us and the burning field was a fourteen-foot stepladder. Lashed to the ladder with rope was Stanley's body. He was tied at the armpits and waist, a shadow before the light. I could make out the LawnsByKnox logo on his sweatshirt. I could see the whites of his sneakers' sidewalls.

At first, I thought his head was just slumped forward onto his chest. But Rimmy ran toward the ladder, and stopped halfway and started to scream, and it was then I could see that Stanley wore no head at all. Dot dropped to her knees and fell on her side. She'd fainted away, and it was all too much. I closed my eyes and tried to breathe, and the wall of flames danced like a tree and warmed my shut eyelids.

It was me who went to the Huntington morgue that Friday. The mortician tried to give me trouble since I wasn't blood kin, but I whispered what I knew about life and death in his ear and he quit protesting quick, and took me to the back. I could see he was doped up just to make it through the day. So many were in that time.

I saw Stanley's face when the mortician pulled back the sheet, and I nodded my head in accordance. I saw Stanley's brain on the stainless steel tray, and its map of folds whispered quiet promises about suns I could hold in my hands.

I stepped out the front door of the morgue and lit a cigarette. It was cold.

* * *

There was a commotion at the bus depot across the street. Two men argued and pointed their fingers while a child stood by and waited. Above them, the striding steel greyhound was pale as a jug of bleach. At night, the greyhound glowed red. In daylight, she disappeared.

I knew we'd stay on the mountain forever then. I didn't care what happened in Mosestown or Huntington or New Orleans or Baltimore or Nome or Port Harcourt or Damascus or Karachi or Yokohama. That world was finally gone to me. Were I to live in it any longer, I would have to kill again, and killing is something that never truly ends, so I would not speak nor write nor think the name Turnbuck ever again. I'd outrun my own end, same as it ever was, same as it ever shall be, amen.

I stared at the pale striding greyhound and envisioned all we'd need to build: the high roosting perimeter towers, the locked shed, the whistles round our necks. I saw row after row of half-runners. I heard the sound of water running out of rock.

We would bundle up and go, all the people of our flock.

SONG OF THE
GREAT HORNED OWL

Once upon a time there was a great horned owl. Her name was Odetta.

Odetta's mother and father raised her with love and attention. They marveled at her physical strength and agility, and they worried at her refusal of hugs and lullabies. They let her fly from the nest at two months old so long as she promised to come back, and she promised, and kept her word. At six months, when a kettle of turkey buzzards came overhead, she turned her wings out, and puffed up, and made herself four times as big. She stared into the eyes of each of the buzzards as they passed. Using telepathy, she said to each of them: "Fuck around and find out."

On her first birthday, when—as instructed—she closed her eyes to make a wish, here is what she thought: I wish I will whip Big Linda's ass before I turn two.

Big Linda was a turkey vulture up back of Sulfur Creek Hollow. She had a tattoo on the side of her head, pinecone on fire. They said one time during the lean year, Big Linda stood in a wake around the mostly bones carcass of a big ole buck, and when two buzzards started fussing over who got first crack at the smidgen of hindquarter meat, Big Linda had hopped onto the dead deer's femur and gripped her talons tight and spread her wings wide and lifted, rocketing up with that femur, which was connected to the pelvis bone, vertebrae, scapula, and skull. They say that buck was fourteen-point, twisting like a wind chime as Big Linda rose higher and higher. She climbed to 20,000 feet. She lined herself up over Big Shoe Rock, a flat scalp of stone big as a barn. She opened her talons. The bones fell.

They say the sound was like a firecracker thunderstring, twelve strip. And after the echo, Big Linda just descended, and landed soft, and began to sweep the scatter into a pile, on which she stood and waited for the rest of them to come, and they did come, and she charged them a dollar apiece for a length of marrowbone, two bucks for a bit of meat. They paid, though it pained them to do so, for it was still six days to Friday, when their checks would come in again.

One sunny day, when Odetta was twenty-three months old, a titmouse she knew name of Greg come round to say Big Linda was at it again and had just dropped a bobcat carcass on Big Shoe Rock, and folks was already lining up, rubbing their nickels together in an orderly queue.

Odetta spat out her jerky and dropped her dumbbells to the wet roost floor. "Let's bounce," she said.

She came in hot at Big Shoe Rock, with only Greg behind her. The turkey buzzards laughed at little Greg and one of them asked why he didn't go back to the low branches where he came from. Odetta paid no mind to any of that. She strode to the front of the line where Big Linda sat in a webbed folding lawn chair with aluminum bones and green armrests.

"How do, Linda," Odetta said.

Big Linda did not look up from her pink pillow cushion, where she sorted money into two piles: the kind that folds and the kind that clinks. "Don't forget the Big," she said.

"How's that?"

"Don't forget the Big. You called me Linda but you forgot to say Big."

Odetta sighed. "I don't truck in lofty nomenclature," she said.

And still Big Linda did not look up from her count. She spoke as she added, eyes on a $2 bill she suspected to be counterfeit: "What is it you truck in, peasant?"

And without missing a beat, Odetta answered. "Ass whippin."

It was then that Big Linda raised her red-inked head and met the yellow-black eye of the young Odetta, whose pupils exploded like perfect black planets, quills rippling with fire. Those eyes were the last thing Linda ever saw, for Odetta was done talking. She had no use for small talk, no use for folks like Linda who would wield their strength to starve their own. Odetta gripped the caprock so hard her talons left behind eight white cuts, and she swiveled at the hips and brought her right wing around in haymaker fashion. The first strike would be the only strike and it blinded Linda. Her lawn chair folded upon itself as it tipped. Her pillow cushion spat out like a tongue, coins catching sunlight as they flipped, paper notes flapping on mountain wind.

Linda lay on her side, trying to make sense of her dead black burning sight. Odetta climbed atop her big buzzard wing and gripped hard. She opened her beak and bent and closed it around Linda's sunburnt neck, two perfect points pressed at the edge of everything. She whispered as she gripped. "You're a lucky bird. I might have opened your throat and spilled your blood, but then the breadline children would have nightmares, wouldn't they?"

And Linda was allowed to leave with the assistance of a hummingbird guide, who was steady at her side, warning of stumps and crevices. And little Greg remade the bobcat's bone shards and meat scraps into piles based on length and girth, and the birds were called forth alphabetically by last name, and all got marrow and sinew enough to carry on until another new day came, and Odetta stood straight and looked them all in the eyes and promised them that the next new day would be better than the one before.

At dawn the new day came. The buzzards mumbled and milled about in the dry grass. When Odetta descended and took her perch upon the sycamore stump, they gathered and addressed her as Your Highness and El Jefe. She raised her wing in response. "I don't truck in lofty nomenclature," she said. "Call me Odetta."

I have always felt fire in my quills.

SONG OF REGRET

My own greatest regret is not one you're liable to guess. It is not a dead settler nor a confederate whose throat I cut. No slavetrader rankles my dreams, no murderer haunts my meditations.

My greatest regret is how I treated that little rich boy on the float plane to Mykonos. I don't know what it did to him, my cruelty, but it surely did something. For so long I tried to find him. His quivered lip came for me again and again, in my dreams and in the Arrow, and in the sky and the window and the wall. I could not have foreseen what would come of my calls to him. It is a tale too strange even for me. But I will tell it.

It's important first to agree upon something basic: A child does not select their parentage. Some are born to those with plenty and some to those without. That child over there has two. That child has one. Now this other one here, he ain't got none. I had no father but I did have a mother. I don't say much on her. She helped Aunt Jane keep me fed for ten years, but I mostly remember my mother as someone who stood around staring at things. She'd stare at a wood knot for an hour. She'd stare down at her cracked hands and rub hogfat on the knuckles. She rarely spoke. My mother wasn't much more than a ghost.

That boy on the plane didn't choose his station any more than he chose his slick-haired daddy with a snake for a tongue, his dumbass mama with her pedicured claws. That boy was only just touching a pane of glass, opening a window his parents had bookmarked, a video of me, which they watched so that they might feel less dead. Hearing my own voice like that in the belly of an iron bird, filled with guilt like I was back then on account of selling my soul for money, it all swirled with the Bombay gin and got my hackles up. But I do not send to know for whom the pelt hackles. The pelt hackles for me.

It wasn't the boy to whom I was whispering threats, and it certainly wasn't thee.

How vast was my regret for getting rich and fat in the way that we did it back then. It had stacked in my chest, my throat, the black folds of my brain. The truth was that anybody could wake up and find themselves a sellout, because money was god almighty and a little taste could put you on a floatplane over the Aegean Sea, trekking 5,000 miles just to hear yourself speak.

I have worn many names in my time. Been different people. But that day I saw my true self on the tablet glass, and then I looked down at my hand, resting as it was pon the folding tray table on the seatback in front of me, and I knew it was the hand of an impostor. You know who's real and who's not when you hear your own voice at 20,000 feet. I was the one on the child's screen.

I needed to put my tray in an upright position. I needed to stretch my legs.

Afterward, straightaway, I knew what I'd done. That night in the Greek choky was when the regret rooted up. And later, in my hammock on the big tramp tanker that ferried me home, I stared at the cargo net above my head, sagged as it was with fifty-five-gallon drums stamped in black: *Bulk Extra Virgin First Cold Press.* I read those words again and again on that three week trip. I said them aloud. I prayer-chanted. *Bulk Extra Virgin First Cold Press Bulk Extra Virgin First Cold Press Bulk Extra Virgin First Cold Press* and in between chant bursts, I cried over how the little boy's lip had trembled. I marveled at how cruel I'd been. I thought of my grandbabies and of Memphis Tennessee Knox. The mass in my throat grew. I was nearly choked when the beautiful tanker captain appeared at my side. He had the kind of jaw and five o'clock shadow you only saw in a magazine at the dentist's. "I wish for you to sign my book," he said, "but first I wish to make you feel better."

It was hard to get the words out, but I did, in a whisper. I said, "There's a plum seed stuck in my throat."

He stood on tiptoe then, and reached so high I couldn't see. He lifted from the net one of the massive yellow drums, and set it on the floor by his feet.

I whispered, in the manner of Mama Klump, "Herculees Herculees."

He took from his belt a chrome bung wrench and spun open the big drum's plug, and he reached inside with his finger and thumb. "Got one," he said and fished out something tiny and orange. He took my hand and opened my palm and put it there. The pill was round and thick, stamped at the middle with the outline of a llama. I set it upon my tongue.

The kind and beautiful captain who never told me his name gave me water then through a bamboo straw and rubbed my forehead with the back of his hand until I'd drunk the bottle down and washed away the seed of the plum, until I'd settled and breathed in rhythm, until the waters of the Strait of Sicily lapped the port windows and threw them open, and filled my hammock with swirling kelp. I floated and spun and entangled my hands in the weeds of the sea, and Cap spun beside me on a purple innertube and remarked, "We call that green algae there the Dead Man's Fingers," and I laughed and laughed and laughed, and I told ole Cap how much I truly loved him. I said: "I mean it, Cap. I mean to say right here and now that I love you to the moon and back."

"I love you more," he said, and then he was gone.

And then I was in New York for three days before I hitched a ride home in a blue custom motorhome piloted by a family of progressive evangelicals from Maine. They didn't ask me one single time if I'd heard the good news. They didn't ask me a thing besides "Where you headed?"

"Mosestown," I said. I slept the whole way home.

Covid came upon us then.

In December of 2022, I told Auntie Eel about the rich boy on the plane, and she understood my regret, and she said, "I know a man can track that boy down for a ten stack," but then came the big storm, and then came the flood, and Auntie Eel was gone. And then Stanley too. Then came fourteen years of untamed life here on Buckwheat Mountain. So many have died, but not yet me. I have slept and I have awakened to write down all of my dreams. I have called out song and signal.

* * *

One night not too long ago, I told Rimmy Knox about the boy on the plane, about how I called to him on my porch roof spectacular. He said to be patient, that it might be working, that he was doing his own calling, only from higher up, and with a bigger rig. He'd been trying to contact Stanley, he said, and his parents and Memphis too, and then he got a far-off thoughtful look in his eye and said he reckoned the living were easier to reach than the dead. I reckoned he was right. He told me, "I have a special frequency might get your job done."

Rimmy took me to the westernmost tower of Freon's perimeter line. I followed him up the ladder with eighty-four rungs and stepped inside. Four telepathic-telegraph machines were lined on a shelf in the corner, and from each ran a strip of copper to the corrugated roof, where lunar panels hummed in tune with the song of Rimmy Knox. "Listen," he said, and I did. He helped me to tune my ear and sharpen the pitch of my hum. We sat on the wet floor of our roost, fingers tapping code on the keys of his machine. "Come to me, boy," I hummed. "Come here to me."

I don't know how many nights we spent in that tower. I do know something strange comes over a human animal who engages in such ritual.

I remember the wind was brisk through the lookout's open half. I watched a stinkbug traverse the knuckle of my tapping hand. Rimmy said, "Hey, look here." He'd spotted something. There was reverence in his voice. "Look at this," he said, and handed me his binoculars.

I couldn't see a damn thing.

* * *

Rimmy pointed. "I bet that's him, moving east between the humps."

It took a minute but I found him, midair, five hundred yards out, just before he touched down on Big Shoe Rock.

He was a man now. He was a flying man.

I watched him—tiny through the lens—as he stretched his long legs on the caprock. He stepped to the edge and spread his dark wings. He bent at the knees and leaped, aimed straight for me. He soared in a line over the ridge, came in hot, and touched down running on the ballfield's slashed stick weeds. "How do!" he called out as he ran. "How do!"

He tripped on a milkweed stalk and went down on his goggled face. He popped right up and hollered, "I'm okay!" Tapped his leather helmet with his fist. "Hard-headed!"

We climbed down the tower's eighty-four rungs, Rimmy and I, and went to meet the young man on the pitcher's mound. He was tall and strong in his discombobulating suit. I could not see his eyes behind the goggles. "How do, Betty Baach!" he said. He stepped inside my personal circle. There was a tingle in my follicles.

He hugged me tight and said, "I've been waiting for this a long time."

I patted his shoulder. We stepped back from each other. I really wished he'd take off those goggles.

He said, "I was stoked to get your message on the frequency."

"You get that station?" Rimmy asked.

* * *

"I get every station." He held out his hand for Rimmy to shake. "Call me Toothpick," he said.

"All right, Toothpick."

His helmet was red leather and his goggles silver. I told him he looked like Burt Lancaster in *The Gypsy Moths* but he didn't know the film. I asked him: "What's this wild getup you got on?"

"I call this my Squirrelygig," he said, and just as easy as you please, he unzipped a long front panel and pulled aside his briefs and whipped out his john longfellow and took a leak, right there for all to see. "Ahhhhhhhhhhhh," he said.

Rimmy looked at me sideways and we cleared our throats and communicated telepathically about the glory of the newly turnt sweetgum leaves.

Toothpick gave it two good shakes and zipped back up. "Funny that you're considering the sweetgum," he said, "for my own testes are spiked like sweetgum seeds."

Rimmy said, "You're a thought reader?"

"I told you I get every station."

I pointed out that, technically, Toothpick's testicles would not be spiked like sweetgum seeds, but sweetgum seed*pods*. I said: "It is important to keep your botanicals sharp, children. It may save your life someday."

Toothpick said, "Touché," though the conversational juncture did not call for such a remark. He told us all about his suit as we walked to the trading post.

* * *

It was a spectacular maroon-and-white wingsuit that he'd sewn together himself out of parachute scraps and coat hangers and raccoon bones. He'd worked on it for years. "I made it in the old ways, like the old-timers right here in the Appalachians," he said. He pronounced it Appalayshuns, but I didn't mind. He pointed to some straight-line stitching under his armpit. "Each panel is sixteen by one with its own air intake hole."

For a man who read minds, Toothpick sure did talk a good bit. He said, "I started looking for you just as soon as I lit out from the old life in '27. I fell in with some traveling evangelicals for a while, and after that I hitched to Mosestown, saved a little money working at the ink factory for eleven months, and then I got on the road with the birdmen."

I did a little math in my head. He'd been seven years old when I met him on the plane. Fourteen when he first ran away. Twenty-five that day he flew onto the mountain.

He said he cut his flying teeth in Mosestown. Said he'd jump off the East End cable-bridge tower and glide just above the black river water, like a giant flying squirrel, disappearing into the slag haze and the sludge fog and the vaporous shifting mists above the tannery ooze.

"How about that?" I said.

"You talk like a poet," Rimmy said. He was walking a circle, sizing the manchild up, sniffing the air around him where he stepped.

I began to wonder where everyone was. "How come nobody's around?" I asked Rimmy. "Where are the children? Where's Dot?"

* * *

He only shrugged and continued sniffing the air. "You smell trans-mission fluid?" he asked me.

"Just one sec," Toothpick said, and he stopped in the field at the outskirts of the post. He undid his whole suit and the long johns underneath, and he dropped them to his ankles, and squatted on the stickweeds, and right then and there, he took a dump. "Unnnnnnnnnnghhhhh," he said.

Me and Rimmy walked on ahead. "Are you wearing your whistle round your neck?" I asked him in a whisper.

He felt at his chest through his ragshirt. "No," he whispered back. "You?"

I was not. I asked him "Do you have the key to the Red Shed on you?"

"No," he whispered. "I lost it."

Toothpick caught up to us by the small fire pit, all zipped up again. He took off his goggles, wore the face of man. Took off his gloves. His fingers were blue.

Rimmy pointed. "Your fingertips are blue," he said.

Toothpick answered quick. "Permanent. From my days at the ink factory."

I sat and stoked the little embers. I looked at his eyes. "Your eyes are blue," I said.

He sat down across from me on a river rock painted in butterflies. He didn't respond to my remark about his eyes. He stretched his long legs and crossed them at the ankle, not an easy feat with the tailribs in the way.

I said, "You get your hands on a pair of those ole color contacts somehow?"

Again Toothpick did not respond. Just sat there with his head down, breathing.

I gave Rimmy the side-eye and a nod of the head. I wanted to tell him telepathically to find Dot and get to the Red Shed quick, but Toothpick got that station.

Rimmy started walking toward the cabins. He was halfway there when I decided to quit drawing things out. I tossed my stick in the pit and watched the blackbone scatter. I stood. I looked down at Toothpick where he sat, his head bowed, his shoulder pads striped in duct tape. I noted an unfamiliar tattoo on the side of his neck. I wanted it all over with.

I made my face as ugly as I could. I said, "Jeewhiz, Toothpick, I sure am awful sorry for how I treated you all those years ago on the floatplane to Santorini."

"Think nothing of it," he said. He did not look up. He sat still as a statue for a minute or more. He shed a tear from each eye but did not move.

He sighed and wiped at his eyes with the back of his blue-fingered hands. Then he growled, cocked his right, and hit himself in the jaw. Took off his backpack, and unzipped it, and pulled out a .38 revolver with white stag grips. He looked at the red embers, pistol limp in his lap. "Let's just quit on all that," he said. And he stood and faced me from across the fire.

I turned my head all the way around but I couldn't spot Rimmy, and there was no one on the hillsides or in the yards or empty picked rows.

He held his gun at his side and thumbed back the hammer. He said, "I figure no one's ever put one in both your eye and your heart all at once."

I told him he figured wrong but I was lying. I asked him: "How did you know to come here like this, to do all this?"

"My name," he said, "is Toothpick Turnbu–"

"Don't you say it, you goddamn son of a bitch."

"You think we don't know morse code? You think we don't have intelligence on every move you've made?"

I'll say this about Toothpick, at that juncture, he was neither focused nor confident. Shifty feet, working his jaw. He was the age of them reared on television and tablet, the ones who'd lost all that roundabout the time they hit twenty-one years of age. Toothpick had watched too much television as a boy, and he grew into a man who spoke accordingly. Cop shows were in his blood.

He said, "You wouldn't think it to look at her but ChrissyJo got a mind like a steel trap."

* * *

"Need to clean your traps," I told him. "You got a raggedy ole dried-out muskrat nest gumming up the works."

He asked me why I'd let ChrissyJo live and I said it was my new thing.

He laughed a real strange and nervous laugh. He reminded me a good bit of Brad Dourif in *One Flew Over the Cuckoo's Nest,* only ugly at the core instead of sweet. He wiped at his eyes again, this time with the back of the hand holding the gun and, for a moment, I thought about rushing him, putting him down hard, but I didn't have the energy any longer.

He regarded me. I thought for a split second that he might come out of his spell, but he didn't. He sniffed and spat on the ground and said, "Would you mind telling me how you knew I wasn't the boy?"

"Not at all," I said. "First, you lay it on too thick. You're a hit man, not a lugger. You let out too much rope."

He nodded his head. I could see by his eyes he would try to remember.

"Second, ink factory closed down in '26."

More nodding.

"Third, your eyes are blue, not goldenbrown. I don't know why you took off the goggles."

"I can't stand how they fog up," he said.

* * *

"Fourth, it was Mykonos, not Santorini."

"Damn," he said. "I knew that."

"And the pissing and shitting?" I asked. I took on a scolding tone: "It was unnecessary."

He said that part was ritual, that he had to empty himself before he took a life, and that typically—when subterfuge was called for—such an evacuative practice worked nicely as diversion to confuse the mark. "Besides," he said, "I always have to go to the bathroom when I'm nervous. Never had to kill a woman before." He raised the pistol and aimed it at my heart.

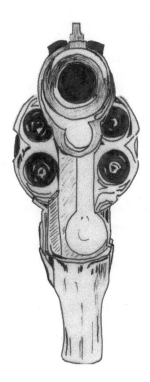

"All right, Toothpick," I said. I could see the copper jackets in the cylinder, poking forth their little heads. I wondered how a dumb piece of shit like Toothpick got his hands on rounds like that. They were worth ten times the gun that held them, which was, incidentally, a perfect sidearm for the likes of Toothpick.

I said: "Smith&Wesson, huh?"

"What of it?"

"Did you lift it from the set of *Octopussy?*"

"What?"

"Barnaby Jones called. He wants his piece back."

"Shut up, you dumb bitch."

"C'mon, Serpico!"

"I said shut the fuck up."

"You got any wine, Uncle June?"

Oh, how I wanted it over with. Oh, how I wanted it done. I watched Toothpick's finger make its way inside the trigger guard. He raised his aim to meet my face. Muzzlehole black as tar. Seablue eye wide open over the sight.

I heard a lion's roar, then a clap of wind.

I saw the kind of yellow light that never has an end.

SONG OF SWITCHBACK

Maybe you once upon a time drove your vehicle down 52 South. Are you old enough to remember? Did you come through McDowell? I believe you did. You may have passed by Freon Hill. You likely drove through ole Kimball and Keystone and Northfork too. You had deep-fried octopus on a stick at Ya'Sou. You paid your respects to the named dead at the World War Memorial. You said out loud you'd try and remember. You had your picture made in front of a great big sign honoring the Northfork High School Blue Demons, who won eight consecutive state basketball titles, 1974–81. You drove on through Powhatan and Ennis, and then you came down into Switchback, and your radio went haywire and started chirping like a fox-squirrel death match, and your engine sputtered and died, and the scant light posts went black and night fell like a man through a trap, and every time you blinked your eyes, you saw—squatted right there on the Cadillac's hood, smiling at you through the windowglass—your daddy, or yourself-only-younger, or yourself-only-older, and each blink was the thumbing of a page in a flipbook you'd glued together that time you sat with god in the tastefully wallpapered living room, that time god asked you to tell the story of your life.

You remember that wallpaper's pattern in god's living room? It was something else, all those redbirds and blackbirds and needles pulling thread.

I have awakened every day for months inside this Cadillac of yours, but I'm the only passenger, and I'm seated at the wheel. I sleep without dreaming and then I awake, sweaty against the red-leather headrest, compelled to remain here behind windowglass in the parking lot of the dead-empty post office. I look in my rearview and catch a glimpse of my grandbabies, but when I spin around there's nothing there. Sometimes it's Memphis in the rearview. Sometimes it's Memphis and Magnolia together, laughing and trading little things I cannot make out. Sometimes it's Eel back there, sometimes Stan. No matter who it is, they are gone when I turn my head to look.

I roll the radio's volume knob and thumb its tuner too. Not a station in range, just waves of static built to crash.

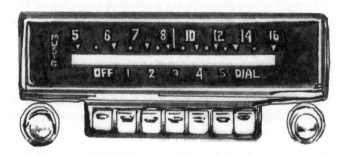

In my lap is a big staple-bound flipbook with a stub pencil holstered snug in a lash of leather. I believe I have written to you every day for months inside this flipbook, inside this Cadillac, inside this post-office parking lot tucked in a switchback turn in Switchback, bent at peculiar angle betwixt creek and road.

I smell burnt transmission fluid. I hear water rolling over rock.

Déjà vu, when you feel it, is teaching you something. You've just got to bend your ear, tune your spork. Try waggling your ears, working your jaw. If you practice enough, you'll get that station.

I am trying to tell you everything about everything.

SONG OF THE SPLINTERCAT

Look there. The children are crouched in the middle of the half-runner rows. They are hiding. The beans are big, most of them ready to harvest. The seeker calls out ready or not, here she damn well comes.

"Don't jostle the stakes," I whisper to the children of the beans. "And pick some damn food while you're out there, fill up your pockets." But the children can't hear my whisper. They're thirty yards away.

Which poet wrote about the pockets of our greatcoats? What were the pockets full of? I don't remember anymore, but I know this for certain: we are lucky to be alive. We could be trapped in a Cadillac on Route 52. We could be underground, running desperate through intricate tunnels filling quick with mustard gas. We could be prefacing our suicide notes, cyanide tucked in the nest of a cigarette's recessed filter. Don't forget to put a little piece of tape over the hole. Don't forget to bring your witness eyes, your wild hands too. You're going to need them all if you want to make it through.

I don't think the playing children want to hear about poetry right now. It seems to me that they never want to hear about poetry.

What chair is this I'm sitting in? What scars mark its arms? Where is my folding aluminum lawn chair? Whose blanket wraps my bones?

It seems to me that this is how it goes most days of late. I awake wrapped in this great big afghan, here in this chair on the lawn, and I can't hardly move a muscle. I can turn my head only a little, lower my eyes to make out the carvings on the arms. I can talk in a whisper. I can see the garden and the woods and the ridge. I cannot see what's behind me. I would give up a finger for a rearview mirror.

The children are always playing a game in the garden. Sometimes it's hide-and-seek and other times mumblety-peg. Sometimes, like today, the half-runners are ripe and green, ready to pick and string. Other times, it's nothing out here but empty turnrows sprouting empty crooked stakes, like the big gray fossil of a water-lynx tail. Sometimes it's so cold you can see your breath on the air. Other times I break a sweat. Leaves on the trees, leaves on the ground. Two or three times, the ripe beans were pink. Once, every row ran purple-red with castor-bean stalks, and on that day I tried to yell to the children: "Be careful! It's poison!" The wind was blowing east and they heard not a thing.

This is how it always goes. I get in a riled state over thinking on weather and crops and poets and outrunning torture with poison and, inevitably, somewhere behind me where I can't see, some polite young adult notes the agitation in my neck and head, and they come on over, and they crouch down next to my chair. They put their hand on mine but it's through the blanket, no skin to skin. What this means is that I can't use the bad prize. I can't even turn my head to look at their eyes.

Always, they say the same damn thing: "Medication time."

This tickles me every time. Que cliché, no? I have a repertoire of lines I whisper back.

I say: "Nurse Ratched, I want *MY* cigarettes!" I scream in a whisper: "I want something done! I want something doooone!"

* * *

But it doesn't matter what I say. The script on the other end is always the same.

"Oh, Evry. You know you have to take your medicine."

"Is my medicine orange? Does it have a llama stamped on it?"

"Please open up now."

"This afghan made of elephant hide? Thing must weigh fifty pounds."

"I don't want to force it down your throat."

"I don't want to bite off your fingers."

"I'm going to put this on your tongue. Stick out your tongue, Winny."

"I'll stick out my tongue when you call me by name, just like every other pauper on my walk. I'll stick out my tongue when you tell me where Rimmy and Dot are."

"Please stick out your tongue."

"What happened to Toothpick? How many slugs did he put in me? Did they lodge or go clean through?"

"Stick out your tongue, please."

"How long was I out? What day is today?"

*   *   *

That last one they'll always answer. I've learned they are happy to oblige questions about current time and date. Come rain or shine or snow or heatwave, they always say the same damn thing.

"Why, it's Christmas Eve of course! Tomorrow is Christmas Day! Open up and say ahhh."

I always try my best to shout before I must bite off the fingers: "Children! What's that skulking in the woods? What's that lurking pon yonder branch? Look up, it's the moon! Look up, it's full of stars!"

And the young adult stands beside me, fixing to tilt back my head. And today is the day I will relent. I will not fight. I won't yell at the children, for I know they will always look up, and I want to look up too because I know now what grace awaits me there. Today I will put everything I have into helping, into tilting my head just as far back as it will go. I'm ready.

One hand grips a hank of my hair and another touches my Pearly-kissed throat. The voice of the hands says to open wide.

I put everything I have into throwing my head back just as far as I'm able.

There is a magnificent crack in my neck, like a hickory trunk in high wind, but I feel no pain. There are no jolts inside me, no light bursting through. My face is pointed at the sky. I have done it. I am splintercat. They can cleave me but they'll never chop me down. Half of me is underground.

*   *   *

I can see the Arrow in the night sky above. It is too big to describe and it is made of stars. I knew it would come back. I can see everywhere it points. I can see the moon. I can see that lucky old sun, rolling around heaven all day. I can see the shapes of fish and birds, and I can see the fishbirds. I know they'll bear witness to future time, long after we are gone. Behind them is a constellation of every tree, and the mule and the oxen too. There's Larry, Pearly, and Odetta, all in an arc. Side-hill gouger, billdad, squidicum-squee.

I see nests of starworms bursting open, blooming, forming pictures of everyone I've known. It is a new kind of likeness, a new level of sight. It is stereotelegraphic and kaleidoscopic and telepathic-kinetic. It is not a suitable sight for those filled with ignorance or fear. It is a sight for the sore eyes of witness.

See how my people dance with the catfish, undulating like sting-rays? See the fishbirds, too, and all those needles pulling their tails of thread? See how the needles jump with every tap of your toe on the glass-bottom roof? Keep tapping. Start your hum and get out your drum.

I hear the measures of the birdsongs stacking now. I hear the cat-erwauling bugs, their little legs sawing. Not a moped in earshot, not a jackhammer in range. I could listen to this kind of music forever. I could watch this kind of dance on the sky all night. I could sit here and look up until tomorrow and the next day and the one after that.

I will. I'll do just that. I will sit here as long you let me. I will lie down with little lambs for as long as it takes, and you can rest your weary head on my bosom.

It won't be hard. I am the Everywhen Woman and I hear the old songs now. There'll be no more bad luck and trouble. There'll be peace in the valley and nothing but freedom on the hill. I know what layers I've took. I am the master of ceremonies to all forms of truth, and I got nothing left in me but love. We can listen shoulder to shoulder to the sound moving through our chambers and caves. Bend your ear. Can you hear the birdsong in the blood? I believe it's the worm-eating warbler. Just listen and try to remember. I won't question your method or catalog your style, for such things are meaningless in this life. We are the same. Your blood is mine and mine is yours, and the truth is that we are trees, and we are llamas and birds and water and fish and fire and coal ash. The truth is, I'm very much in love with you.

Here is a bandolier lashed with everything you'll need. When midnight is nigh, uncork your desert canteen. Inside is lightning. It's the old one-batch hooch, and it will hollow your bones and set you soaring free. You'll need just four or five slugs to answer the radial call of the core of love, and this is what you'll proclaim: *I am ready at any time. Do not keep me waiting.*

They say most people fly up to 20,000 feet and stop, and hover, and take one last look down below. They say this world is beautiful from up there. I hope I get to see it. I hope I get to hold my own bones in my hands and drop them for the ones still on the ground. I'll be light as a feather when I watch them land, and you'll be floating beside me, and I'll reach for your hand.

I'll wink at you then, one last time. We'll aim ourselves like rockets and count down from nine. We'll fly at light speed to that lucky old sun, and in the picked-clean teeth of the unknown gods, at last, we will have begun.

ACKNOWLEDGMENTS

When I was a younger writer, I read "For the White poets who would be Indian" by Wendy Rose. I have participated in the temporary tourism of souls that Rose calls out in that poem. As a writer and as a human being, I have tread on artistic and other ground that wasn't mine to tread on. As I've evolved, I've tried to reconcile this by facing the history of this land's Indigenous peoples. I have a long way to go. In retrospect, my notions of the myriad, enduring, and often terrifying realities of Black people in America have similarly been weak, and my work similarly insufficient. But I have been listening a while now to this nation's true past. It is a colonial and genocidal one, an entity built on the enslavement, oppression, policing, and killing of Black people, and it works steadily and intricately to swindle all poor and working people. I hope this book offers honor, respect, love, and fortification for all who are oppressed or misrepresented.

I hope too that, although I am not a woman, Betty's stories were suitable to tell in the manner I've told them here. She was a voice that I listened to and tried to put on paper. Her sound comes from so many different women. Some of them I have known: Dot Jackson, my Grandma Lena. Some of them I have only read. There are two writers in particular whose voices influenced every note in this book. First, as always, was Louise McNeill. From Sol Brady's shadow to her particular telling of John Brown's hanging, she is here once again, and I am continually grateful.

Moreso even than Louise McNeill, this book's most profound influence was Lucille Clifton. I had the great fortune to be in her presence once, in 1992, in my hometown of Huntington, West Virginia. She'd come to give a reading at Marshall University, and

I was young and stupid and did not realize then whose legendary hand I was shaking, whose eyes I had the privilege of meeting with my own. I have turned to Lucille Clifton so many times over the years for help in figuring how to live. She endured and endured, and she remembered and imagined and dreamed and wrote with such truth and precision and particular bone-and-blood music that I am forever in awe. As we've watched the acceleration of this country's most cruel, racist, and nationalist inclinations over the past several years, I have returned to and read the entirety of Lucille Clifton's work, including *Generations*, a memoir that is—like McNeill's *The Milkweed Ladies*—one of the most important pieces of writing in existence. Lucille Clifton is everywhere in these pages, from the witness eye and wild hands to the memory of the birds and the sounds of the children. I could never express my gratitude for the work she made, and I can only tell others to read it right away, and to support artists and sanctuaries of light like Clifton House in Baltimore.

I hope that readers will also find—despite all noise of hate and fear—the love and light we have here in Appalachia. I hope that the true history of our people gets told. I would like to acknowledge the work of two particular historians who are bringing light to the important history of Black experiences in our shared hometown of Huntington, West Virginia. These historians are Ancella Bickley and Cicero M. Fain III. You will find their influence in these pages, in such things as a character's name or a riverside setting. I consulted Bickley's *Memphis Tennessee Garrison: The Remarkable Story of a Black Appalachian Woman,* as well as Fain's *Black Huntington: An Appalachian Story.*

I hope that readers might seek out real and contemporary Appalachian voices of resistance instead of tired tales that rely on excavation and predictable distortions. There is much good recent work—artistic, community-based, otherwise, and in-between—being done by enduring folks nearby, and I'll just give you a few: the Appalachian Prison Book Project, the STAY Project, and Higher Ground. I must give particular acknowledgment to Robert Gipe, who allowed me to live and write in his Harlan, Kentucky, home for thirteen days in May of 2018. He is a true BucketMouth of TalePackia, and in addition to his work with Higher Ground and other programs, his trilogy has been immeasurably influential and important to me and to so many others who are writing and making art in these hills. Thank you, my friend, for everything.

Oh, Captain, My Cousin, Ann Pancake. Thank you.

I am grateful to *Iron Horse Literary Review* for publishing "Song of the Great-Horned Owl" in issue 23.2, the Power Issue; and I am grateful to *Huizache* for publishing "Song of the Panther" in issue 9, Fall 2022.

Many thanks to all the good folks at UMass Press, particularly Courtney Andree, Rachael DeShano, Sally Nichols, and Deste Roosa.

Shoutout to old friends from the H whose family names I took up herein. Stephen Hornbuckle from way back, and Pete Rivas, also from way back, and beyond. And for the likenesses in the tree photographs, many thanks to Ben Shahn, Dot Jackson, Patricia Brown, Memphis Tennessee Garrison, Aunt Marilyn, Pete Rivas, Ancella Bickley, Dad, Mom, Carrie & Lisa, Jason Williams, and Lump.

Shout out to the following entities, alluded to inside these pages. Films: *It's a Wonderful Life, 2001:A Space Odyssey, Rikki-Tikki-Tavi, Octopussy, Serpico, Friday, Cool Hand Luke, The Sting, The Nutty*

Professor, The Gypsy Moths, and *One Flew Over the Cuckoo's Nest.*
Television shows: *Avatar: The Last Airbender, Saturday Night Live*
("Sprockets"), *The Sopranos,* and *Barnaby Jones.* Songs: "Robots" by
Dan Mangan, "That Lucky Old Sun" by Ray Charles, "Peace in the
Valley" by Sam Cooke and the Soul Stirrers, "Bless the Telephone"
by Labi Sifre, and "Baguetti" by Smino. Book: *Kickle Snifters and
Other Fearsome Creatures* by Alvin Schwartz and Glen Rounds.
People: John Brown, Lucy Parsons, Studs Terkel, Hal Greer, Fat
Lever, Larry Bird, Johnny Eck, Bill Withers, Doris Payne, Frank
Stowers, Philip Seymour Hoffman, Brian Collins ("Boom Goes
the Dynamite"), Prince, Seamus Heaney, Maxine Cumin, Wilfred
Owen, Amiri Baraka, James Still, and Sappho.

I wrote most of this book in the basement, and I'd come up and
read its wild passages to my family. For listening, and for offering
your good thoughts, I thank you, Margaret, Reece, Parsley, and
Eli. You are my light and my everything. I'm very much in love
with you.

JUNIPER
JUNIPER PRIZE FOR FICTION

This volume is the twenty-fourth recipient
of the Juniper Prize for Fiction,
established in 2004 by the
University of Massachusetts Press
in collaboration with the
UMass Amherst MFA Program
for Poets and Writers, to be
presented annually for an outstanding
work of literary fiction. Like its sister award,
the Juniper Prize for Poetry established
in 1976, the prize is named in honor
of Robert Francis (1901–1987),
who lived for many years at
Fort Juniper, Amherst, Massachusetts.